THE MOONLIGHT IN GENEVIEVE'S EYES
and Other Tales of Horror

I0548056

Copyright © 2024 by D. Krauss
First Published 2007

SECOND EDITION
Published October 2024
By Indies United Publishing House, LLC

Illustrations by Cassandra Harris

All rights reserved worldwide. No part of this publication may be reproduced, distributed, or transmitted in any form or by any means, including photocopying, recording or other electronic or mechanical methods without the prior written permission of the publisher, except in the case of brief quotations embodied in critical reviews and certain other non-commercial uses permitted by copyright law.

This book is a work of fiction. References to real people, events, establishments, organizations, or locales are intended only to provide a sense of authenticity, and are used fictitiously. All other names, characters, places and incidents in this publication are fictitious or are used fictitiously, are drawn from the author's imagination and are not to be construed as real. Any resemblances to real persons, living or dead, events or locales is entirely coincidental

This ebook is licensed and may not be re-sold or given away to other people.

Free copy: This book remains the copyrighted property of the author and may not be redistributed to others for commercial or non-commercial purposes.

ISBN 978-1-64456-761-6 [Hardcover]
ISBN 978-1-64456-762-3 [Paperback]
ISBN 978-1-64456-763-0 [ePub]

Library of Congress Control Number: 2023943096

INDIES UNITED PUBLISHING HOUSE, LLC
P.O. BOX 3071
QUINCY, IL 62305-3071
indiesunited.net

To Ray Bradbury, who lit the fuse

Table of Contents

Forward..*vi*

The Moonlight in Genevieve's Eyes...............................1
Choice...11
The Flowers in Mr. Williams' Garden...........................29
Cistern..39
The Elvish Woman..57
The Trumpet Inside the Warehouse..............................67
King of the Bears..91
Angel Eyes..107
The Absence of Land...125
Face to Face..133

About the Author...151
OTHER BOOKS BY D. KRAUSS..........................152

The Moonlight in Genevieve's Eyes

Ten Tales of Horror and the Supernatural

D. KRAUSS

INDIES UNITED PUBLISHING HOUSE, LLC

Forward

It isn't the severed head, the gouged-out eye, fangs sinking into your throat that frighten. It's what precedes: a footfall in the dark, a blade *snikking* open, glowing eyes in a corner. Because there's still hope, a chance, that the man in the woods will pass by, the blade is just for trimming fingernails, the eyes merely illusion and you are terrified, terrified, that it isn't so, isn't so, and you will end up...severed.

Here, then, are ten tales of hope.

The Moonlight in Genevieve's Eyes

It's October, Genevieve, October, and you know what that means.

They'll be running the streets in sheets, in sheets the streets, streets, sheets, yes, yes I know, rhymes, I'm caught in them again.

But they'll be in sheets, they will. Delicious. There'll be a moon this year, maybe not full, but a moon nonetheless though I must check, I must check to be sure because you know, Genevieve, how the moon lights your eyes.

Ah, I can see it now. With one or two shots I put out the street light at the end of the driveway and plunge the night, frosty and white, night and white *stop*! plunge it into lovely half-light, so spooky, so spooky, the people in sheets and black capes will look around nervously because they have lost the comfort of sodium glow, the safety of it.

They'll be vulnerable.

Do you remember the first time, Genevieve, the first time we dressed in sheets and ran through the alleys and caught up with your sister and my little brother and we jumped at them and they screamed and screamed and it was so delicious, so fun, we run, fun and run, fun and run and we kept finding them at the ends of the streets because you and I know these ways so well who can stop us, who? and finally they were crying, so afraid, so afraid, and we laughed. We laughed, Genevieve.

We were ten. And your eyes in the moonlight, Gen ...

I have to carve the pumpkin.

It might be too early because there's still September in the air, still too much of the heat that September steals from August and pushes past its borders fooling us all, fooling us because it's too hot, just too hot for October but, wait it's cooling off a bit so maybe, finally, but no, no, warm again. Damn damn damn. So if I get the pumpkin now you know what'll happen, you know, the melting, the scrunching so it looks like an old geezer pumpkin, the bones of its face sagging to a blur and you don't know who it is, you don't recognize him unless you see a picture of him younger then maybe you can recognize the misshapen, wrinkled, smooshed thing he's become.

Like Mr. Gardner. Do you remember him? I saw his picture, Air Corps uniform and smiling and young and looked so devil-may-care, Gen, had a scarf around his neck. Imagine! And unless you saw that photo on his mantel with the blue medal draped over it you would never have known, ever, Genevieve, that it was Mr. Gardner. Old, sour, mean Mr. Gardner who yelled at us and put the hose on you for riding your bike across his lawn.

I saw the picture just briefly, Gen. And he burned, oh did he burn.

I would have loved to see the orange in your eyes.

That was when we were twelve, Genevieve, and I came over and you weren't even dressed yet and I said, hey, are we going, or what? And for a second, just a second, you hesitated and I thought, Genevieve, that you had somehow forgotten and how can you forget Halloween? Just how? And you laughed and said ohmigod a ghost, Teddy, Teddy the ghost and I was pleased when you said 'wait up' and got your sheet and we got the bikes and we were fast, so fast, and there, Mr. Gardner, lumbering on his lawn and you, you jumped the curb! I was so proud, so thrilled and you know, just before he turned the hose on you, just before you rent his roses, you looked at me and there was the moon in your eyes, Gen, there.

I always want to see that.

So, what, I should wait two more weeks, I think, and I will go out to the country and look over fields and pick one, a big one, always a big one because I want everyone to see. The candle has to be big, too, big light, so bright, the only thing in sight for the ghosts and black capes and skeleton boys and little princesses as they stand in the dark under the broken globe trembling a little and there, over there, what's that? The biggest, glowiest, orangiest, scariest pumpkin on the block.

They'll all want to come and see.

Like when we were fifteen, Genevieve, and I had it, the biggest, most orange of them all, sitting on my porch. I put dry ice and a blue candle inside with a glow stick and it was eerie, really eerie and I knew we could scare the kids and make them cry. But what did you do, Genevieve, what did you do? You just looked, you just stood there at the bottom of the driveway and you didn't even come close and I kept saying come here, come here, there's nothing to fear, here and fear, nothing to fear here

But you didn't come, you didn't. You looked at me kinda like you looked at the frog we had to dissect (and you didn't even dissect it with me, did you, no, no you didn't, but with Franklin. Franklin!) and you said, gee, nice, and your eyes were all away, no moonlight in them, and you were not my Genevieve, no you weren't, you were someone else, a junior varsity cheerleader and steady of a football player

(a football player, Gen?)

and you had that face, that face I always got from all the girls and not just the cheerleaders and I knew that face would go somewhere later, the girl's bathroom, and laugh and call names. And you just walked away.

And when I came to your house, you weren't even there.

Oh, Gen, you shoulda seen my fury. I was the white-sheeted fury and I raced on my bike and I hit the alley, spraying puddles and pebbles and there was a full moon, Gen, there was a full moon and I did not get to see it in your eyes. But I did see the kid in the ninja costume at the end of the street.

With a rock, Gen, with the proper application of a rock you just happen to find like it was purposely placed there by the gods of all the carved pumpkins that come alive when the moon, the full moon, is shining down on them, Gen ... you can get a kid down a storm drain. Mostly in one piece.

I will carve the vicious grin, the most malicious grin, just dripping with scorn. I've gotten very good at that, don't you think? And everyone will stand at the end of the drive and crane their necks and be disturbed because I will use the blue candle and the glow stick and the dry ice. They will all want to come closer. They will all want to look.

Franklin standing over me and I am bloody and black-eyed and crying and everyone's laughing at me, all of them as usual but you're there, you're there, too, Gen, and you look down at me and your face is screwed up like an old, heat-shrunk pumpkin and your mouth is open and it's twisted into that same look of malice I have gotten so good at carving and I see, I see, Genevieve, not the moon in your eyes, not the orange. I see something else, Gen.

Contempt.

For me, for me, Gen? Don't you remember the runs through the alleys and the scaring of the little kids and the slingshots at the cats and the ghost bikes tearing such big holes in so many people's yards and you laughing, laughing and we are free and scary and screaming and wet from Mr. Gardner (and he was orange later) and you looked at me with the moon, the silver power of the moon, shining so bold in your eyes? We were of the moon, Gen. And you traded the moon for contempt.

When I got out of the hospital that other time, Gen, I read that you and Franklin were engaged and you were going to some school. Maybe you shouldn't put stuff like that in the papers, Genevieve, maybe you shouldn't because I got upset and stopped taking the medicine. Mom moved out. She did. The state sends a nurse but I can lie, oh yes, 'cause we both learned how together, didn't we?

Can you hear them shuffling up the driveway, Genevieve, drawn by the light because it's so dark on the street now? They all want to look. Oh please let there be a full moon.

So I put on the sheet and had with me the best of my carvers, the very best, so sharp, so precise, for such delicate work.

How many years now, Gen? I'm not very good with time, but I can rhyme, rhyme with time, and climb, in time I can climb and there I am supine and you whine 'what's that noise?' and sublime! the balcony door slid too fine and you, you, the moon in your eyes, divine

I am so fast.

They came to ask me questions but, Genevieve, I can lie.

So maybe I will shoot out the other street light and make the whole place dark so the only attraction, the only thing to see is the big, big orangey pumpkin on my porch, delicious and malicious, and they will shuffle and sidle and look at each other and feel scared, oh, scared, because those eyes, those eyes, they look so real.

And if the moon is up, Gen, if it's there, and if there's

still enough frost from the freezer, you will gleam at them.

Just gleam.

*Original version in *Crime and Suspense,* November, December 2007

Choice

At noon, Toby's master was staked, his head and heart removed, garlic stuffed in the still living mouth, and then the coffin and remains burned. At exactly one minute past noon, Toby collapsed, screaming, in the middle of an insane crowd rushing down Broadway. Everyone stepped around him as he went into spasms vomiting his master's blood. A cop kicked him once, "Get movin', ya junkie asshole," which was a far more accurate statement than the cop knew.

The next week or so, Toby shivered inside a cardboard box in an anonymous alley near the Theater District, vomiting a lot more of the master's blood. The other derelicts kept a wary distance. There is an unholy glow about the damned that the almost-damned perceive so, when Toby blinked himself to a midnight consciousness, took in a ragged breath laced with sobs and tried to remember who he was, he still had his shoes, his coat, and, surprise, his wallet.

And he also had the most ungodly of thirsts.

"Ungh," was his first post-slave utterance, not the most articulate, but probably the best summary of the raging pain melting the inside of his head. A migraine. Great. Those were back. But it didn't compete with the craving, the soul-twisted craving for a taste. Just a taste. Something black and eternal roiled his heart and he smiled, well, bared teeth, remembering the heights, the soaring of his senses and the unlimited depths of cold, unmitigated power. Slavery had its benefits.

He wanted it back.

Toby peered into the gloom with what remained of the night vision the master had imparted. There were various lumps huddled here and there near trashcans. His bared teeth turned into a gloat.

Food.

He leaped up, glad he still retained the heightened speed and strength, even though the motion made his head implode. He was across the alley in a second, snarling, which his master had told him never to do because it was rather undignified. Well. He was wet, covered with about an inch of oil-soaked dirt, had crapped himself several times and had breath that turned the cold air green, so dignity was not an issue. He seized the first lump by the back of the neck and pulled it to its feet. The bum, long-bearded and wild-eyed, uttered a "Wadahell?" and kicked him viciously. That hurt. It actually hurt, and, surprised by that, Toby dropped the bum, who ran screaming from the alley, followed by the other screaming lumps. Toby was too engrossed with the revived sensation of a kick to the stomach to reach out and grab one of them. But he recovered quickly enough and, still snarling, crouched, studying the filth-piled dumpster in front of him. There. A rat. He jumped, yelped as it tore his thumb open, and sank his teeth into its body.

"JEEEEEESSSSUUUS!" a voice called as a light blinded him in mid-bite. He could imagine how he looked, a dirt troll with a rat struggling in its mouth, but the more immediate need was the precious fluid and he snatched the rat to his chest, breaking its neck to stop the biting. He hissed at the intruder. Get your own!

The voice belonged to a college boy dressed in Dockers and a light sweater. A college boy next to him had the flashlight. Another college boy behind the first had a baseball bat. Come to think of it, so did the other two.

"Chewseedat? Chewsee?" the Jesus-caller was in shock, pawing at his two sidekicks.

"Fuck. Ing. Bums!" the first bat wielder emphasized every syllable while slapping the Louisville against a palm. Toby had heard about these guys; an initiation requirement, bring back pictures of the derelicts they worked over, the grosser, the better. Toby was probably about the grossest they'd ever seen.

Ordinarily, Toby would have laughed, trussed them, and left them by the coffin for his master's leisurely draining. But his powers were rapidly diminishing, he was still bothered by pain, and the rat attack had cost him his alliance with the night dwellers. Facing suddenly limited options, Toby ran.

They pursued, and Toby was in trouble. He didn't know where he was and he kept running into dumpsters and other bums and walls, each collision a shock to his newly awakened nerves. Somewhere he lost the rat and he screamed in anguish, even considered going back for it as the boys bore down. He needed a meal to reinvigorate his gifts; then he would bound over the boys' heads and tear them in half, savoring their life force. With his night vision failing geometrically, though, his speed and strength halving every second, his oneness with the night separating, going back for the rat would be suicide. He cursed and ran, pell mell, down the alleys.

"Master," he moaned as he burst onto a dim street, "why didn't you turn me?" Why didn't he? Afraid of the competition?

Feet were gaining and there were whoops of triumph and Toby's night vision was completely gone. He sensed a building at the end of the street and, with a burst of terror-fueled speed, bee-lined for it. He sprang, hit the steps and then realized, too late, what it was.

A church.

The blue fire roared up his leg and encircled his heart. In his agony, Toby saw the college boys standing at the bottom, aghast at the sight of a man burning to death on a concrete landing. Then the blue flame reached high and slapped him hard.

Cold, so cold, so dark

⌣

"Lie still."

The voice was a whisper, a feather brush, and Toby was not sure he'd heard right. He was in a half world of fire and ice; the other world of night and power, the one he loved, was somewhere on the edge and he ran towards it, crying, for what seemed years but it receded like a desert mirage with his every step. He saw the eyes of his master there, mocking while urging him on. In the fire and ice behind him, Someone Else watched, rather dispassionately. Maybe that's who spoke.

There was coolness on his brow and blankets wrapped about him. He was warm, actually warm.

Strange to feel that again. He opened his eyes.

The double and triple blurred images resolved themselves quickly. It was a small, stark room. The walls were beige and cracked, the old plaster framed with dark wood here and there. No ornamentation, except for the plain cross hanging opposite him. He gasped.

"Lie still," the voice repeated, firmer this time so, no, it was not a dream, especially since he felt the blankets being tucked in tighter. He eyed the cross and wondered why he had no urge to flee. He glanced down and saw fingers of sunlight streaking across the blankets and wondered why he did not shudder.

"Do you feel better?" ah, yes, the voice, should see who that was, and Toby looked in its direction. A monk, a brown-wrapped man with a friar's tonsure, clear, light eyes and lines of sorrow for a world gone mad. Caring. Loving. Toby stared. When was the last time he'd seen such a loving face, one that regarded him with the same compassion, the same concern? A year ago, a hundred years ago, a thousand. Mom.

Toby started to cry.

"There," the coolness on his head, a wet cloth, was removed and the friar gently applied it to Toby's aching eyes. So refreshing, it made him cry harder. "It's all right," the friar murmured, "it's all right. Whatever pain or sin drove you here, it is now past."

"Here?"

"The Priory of St. Michael and St. George. We took you here after ..." the friar's voice trailed off and his eyes glazed.

"Who's 'we'?"

"We," was all the friar said.

Okay. No further explanation needed. Monks were basic do-gooders.

"Tell me," the friar leaned over him, a look of wonder on his face, "what was it like?"

"What was what like?" Admit nothing. These church types were pretty free with their garlic and stakes.

"Undergoing the purge of God," and the friar clasped his hands together.

"Excuse me?"

"When I saw it," the friar's voice enraptured and his prayer hands clutched and unclutched, "when I saw you wrapped in Holy Fire, I was, am, so astonished. To have actually seen it!" He began rocking back and forth, like those black-clothed believers at the Wailing Wall. "I am not worthy of it, Lord, not worthy!"

"Uh"

"Tell me!" and the friar swooped, his eyes crazy lights and Toby shrank into the cot. Oh boy, one of those. Toby had to be careful. One slip-up and this could end badly.

So let's play.

"It was cold, so very cold," Toby whispered in his best

approximation of a penitent's voice.

"Yes!" a fanatic's voice, no approximation, "a cold fire! The dichotomies of God!" the rocking began again, followed by lots of praise. Toby relaxed. He was in. Toby stared at the friar's throat moving to and fro, the jugular pulsing there. The black around his heart stirred and there Toby was, on the wind, sniffing the death on it, the prey, the power.

"I," Toby breathed, "thirst."

"Ah," the friar came back to earth, was sympathetic. "Of course. I am sorry but, to be in the presence of a miracle," the friar turned. Toby fixed on his throat. The friar came back with a cup of water, "Here."

"No," Toby shook his head violently. "That's not what I mean. I want ..."

"Yes?"

That throat. A lunge and a tear away. Then life coursing through him, power restored, the night his. Toby's heart raced and he could feel the forever call of something bestial, the soaring, orgasmic rage.

And then, it just spun away.

Toby gasped. "No!"

"What is it?" the friar was concerned.

"It's gone, it's just gone!" desperately, Toby squeezed his shoulders together, trying to touch the black around his heart. It was unresponsive. "I thirst!" he insisted, more to himself than the friar.

"Ah!" the friar nodded. "A sin thirst! You always will. The Justice of God requires a thorn of the flesh. A reminder of your former wickedness."

Toby frowned. That seemed a bit off. You don't call the owl pouncing on the mouse wicked "There's nothing to remind."

"Oh?" the friar turned and poured the water into a basin. How quaint. Toby would have laughed, under other circumstances. "But there has to be, otherwise you would not be favored with God's Fire. Do you not feel the shame of your past?"

"No," Toby said. "It's not like I had much choice."

The friar considered. "Then you were a victim of the wickedness, not its source."

"Well, yeah!" Brilliant flash of the obvious. "I mean, you get grabbed out of your Studebaker and ..." forced to swallow the blood of the undead, sleeping among the rotting bodies tossed carelessly by the master's coffin, feeding from his drippings, stalking the streets in life-sapping daylight to make the purchases and arrange the shipments the master needed to survive in this human world — there's a bit of victimology in that. Probably shouldn't give those details, though. Toby shut up.

"And yet," the friar gently laid the cloth back on Toby's forehead, "at any time, you could have left the wickedness in which you were unwillingly taken."

No, he couldn't. Maybe a stronger man of more

independent will could have dragged the stuporous master from the coffin and into the conflagration of the sun. But not Toby, not with the exaltation of midnight, the hunt, the kill, the sheer lusting joy of it. "You don't understand," Toby said.

"You are right," the friar nodded. "I have spent most of my life in these shelters. What I know of wickedness is only what I have studied. Your experience is foreign to me. But, it is, without a doubt, something you chose."

Toby was astonished. "Choosing a miserable slavery instead of a horrible death makes me wicked?" He'd leave out any mention of the upside.

The friar waved Toby's rising protest down, "Yes, it does. The Fire proves your former wickedness," and the mad lights were back in his eyes.

Toby snorted. "It's not wicked to survive; it's just not, no matter what you have to do. Your God," and he spat that word, "has some rather harsh standards."

"He is your God, too," the friar spoke softly, "and yes, His standards are very hard. They are uncompromising; else He would not be God. But His compassion is also uncompromising. You have been given your life back, through God's own purification. You now have a choice."

"What?"

"To return as you were, or to live a new life."

"With this thirst?" Especially at night?

"Yes," the friar closed his eyes and dropped his head, "as we all thirst, and earn the pure joy of resisting it, through God's strength."

Toby considered. He did, actually, feel pretty good. The migraine was gone and there was an independent strength in his limbs now, not the one he borrowed from the master. He was not bled by sunlight and could now walk proudly in day. Go to a park. Swim in fast-moving water. Pat a black dog with white brows. Eat garlic pizza — Toby laughed inwardly at that. He cast back to prior days, playing football with his cousins on a leaf-tossed hill as autumn descended, Sunday dinners with the pastor discussing the ominous movements of the Japanese, that first kiss with Audrey as the winter's night wheeled above them like a blanket and not a shroud.

But there were other memories. His milksop, mealy-mouthed, migraine-driven powerless life of scraping and bowing and fearing what the boss might say. Being careful around the in-laws should they decide to cut them out of the will. Lusting impotently after scornful, peroxide secretaries.

Go back to that? After running with wolf packs and throwing, with one hand, fat-assed louts across a room? Deliberately picking fights in bars and having the bikers chase him outside and then the sudden terror in their eyes as Toby turned and the master emerged from his hiding place ... give that up?

Uh uh.

Toby eyed the friar balefully. How many fewer assholes, Padre, are now stalking your parish because of Toby and the master? They had actually done good service, one the padre's God (not Toby's) wouldn't. You should be thanking me right now, instead of judging, Toby thought. He grinned.

"Does something amuse?"

Damn. "I'm not laughing," Toby said hastily, "I'm ... considering, yes, considering what this new life will mean for me."

"And?" the friar leaned forward eagerly.

"I mean, it'll be hard, it'll really be hard, you know? You just don't stop doing what I was doing and go back to work, you know? Go back to family. But I'm really willing to give it a try."

"A try?" the friar looked at him askance. "Do you not understand you were given a holy gift?"

"Well, yeah, yeah, it was pretty holy and I feel," no burning at the sun's touch and no quaking fear in the shadow of the cross, "great. Really do, so I think I'm going to be okay."

"You cannot merely try. A man who has been given such a gift must commit to it."

"Huh? How?"

"We need certain assurances," the friar said.

That 'we' again. "What assurances?"

"That you will not return to your wickedness."

"I won't," Toby said but saw immediately the friar wasn't buying it. "Look, seriously, I won't. It was, over all, pretty terrible." He shuddered, remembering the abattoir he lived in, but the shudder was punctuated with some of the black thrill.

"I can imagine," the friar was sympathetic, "and you now have the tools to put the wickedness behind. The Fire purged you. But it is easy to resume past ways."

"I'm not going back to that. No sir, no way," he made to throw a hand out but the blankets wouldn't let him. "That's done. Over. Finito."

The friar stared.

"Look," Toby was getting very irritated, "what do I have to do here? Fall on my knees?"

"You must provide assurance," the friar repeated.

"This is getting a bit circular. What do you need? I can't do much more than tell you I'm okay now, so you're wasting your time. You've got other things to do, I'm sure. Aren't you supposed to be out giving alms or washing feet or something?"

"Ministering to God's creatures comes in many forms," the friar said.

"Okay, well, you've done a really good job here. I mean it, you have. A letter of commendation to the Pope or Friar Tuck or whoever you work for. Seriously,

I'll do that," Toby pushed the sincerity. "I think I just want to get started at it. Yeah, I think that's what I want to do, into the fray, half a league onward, wot? Right now. I want to start right now, so I'm going home. Right now." Screw the friar and his assurances, whatever the hell that was: the night called. Eagerly, Toby pushed but the blankets didn't yield. He struggled against them but they were folded in such a way they only tightened. "Hey!" he said, "what's this?"

"Oh!" the friar threw apologetic hands to his cheeks. "I'm so very sorry! I was afraid you would fall out. You were thrashing about when you were unconscious. Here," he reached down and loosened the blankets.

Toby sat up. "Finally!" He had a good mind to throw the friar across the room. In memory of the master.

The friar bowed his head, "Again, I apologize." He turned to a low cupboard set against the wall and his frock pulled down, exposing his throat and the pulsing life dancing there, mesmerizing

Toby did not know where he was, nor who else was about. He wasn't sure the weaknesses brought on by daylight were completely gone; he could be weaker than he felt. But the master always told him these opportunities were fleeting and you must strike at their first offer. Deal with the fallout later.

He did not snarl this time, he roared. And by the friar's pathetic and powerless God, the strength was full on him, screaming in his blood as he screamed after the friar's, his hands claws and blue, his eyes red and death, his teeth salivating and extending and he lunged ...

And was stopped cold. There was something holding him back. Puzzled, he looked down and saw a halter around his shoulders. He didn't need to turn and see the cord leading from it to the wall — he could feel it.

"Toby." The friar sat calmly, legs crossed under the tunic, relaxed. "That's not very assuring."

Toby screamed and raged and strained but the halter wouldn't budge. He reached behind for the cord and yanked his hand back, howling.

"Soaked in holy water," the friar said.

Toby looked up. The cross grew to the size of an oak and loomed over him, pulsing retribution. He collapsed, holding his hands over his face and scrambling his now smoking legs out of the slivers of sunlight. Toby had spent the last sixty years or so in a state of fear, but only of the master. Now he knew what the master always feared.

"Almost noon, Toby," the friar consulted a wristwatch and looked at him meaningfully.

"How do you know me?" Toby's voice sounded craven, even to him.

"Well, there's your wallet. But, you left quite a few IDs around your master's coffin, too." The friar reached back to the cupboard. "It's too bad, really. You had a chance; you experienced the Fire. But you threw it away, made a bad choice. Now, you give us no other." And he turned back, the stake in his hand. Toby quivered. It was hawthorn.

He screamed. Just once.

*Original version April 2008 issue of *Midnight Times*

The Flowers in Mr. Williams' Garden

They grew in a six-by-six bed in the middle of Mr. Williams' front yard, ornament to an already ornamental lot. Mr. Williams' brick split-level, classically shuttered, classically front-porched, seventy-five years old maybe but well kept, was a pleasing sight in itself, a stand-out in a quaint neighborhood filled with similarly pleasing, large-yarded, brick two-stories-and-split-levels. Great willow oaks grew randomly down the street, one especially large specimen fronting Mr. Williams' eastern boundary, shading and greening and giving an air of settled suburban tranquility, demiurge for wearied city workers.

The flowers added to the tranquility. Clematis, or some kind of subspecies, tall and lush and thick, impenetrable. Each plant stood at least six feet, tightly bound and facing the world with a uniform front of giant red blooms at least seven inches across, yellow pistils waving frantically, a breathtaking sight.

They were never watered, never trimmed, never attended in any way that anyone could remember. Yet they were properly staked, or at least seemed to be, because there was some kind of artificial support among them, glimpsed when the wind moved the plants enough to show some depth. All of this spoke of attendance, but no one knew who attended. Certainly not Mr. Williams.

Certainly no one in the neighborhood.

So arresting a sight always attracted admirers. Cars, exploring the neighborhood for the shortcut it provided between the two main thoroughfares that, in turn, afforded access to the Beltway, often slowed when they approached, especially in winter when all the world was dead and the drivers expected nothing but deadness. Topping the rise, they were confronted by a sea of red, beautiful flowers waving in the breeze and you could almost hear them exclaim as the cars slapped to a halt, "Flowers? In January? How'd they do that?" They'd sit for a while, the tones of pleasure and surprise giving way to quiet as they stared, then they would glance around nervously and shift in their seats and suddenly drive away. They never came back so, if there was one advantage to the flowers, they did hold down the traffic.

Sometimes people would actually get out of their cars to look. The ones merely obtuse, who never took counsel of their unease, would only get as far as the curb before looking about fearfully then hastily driving away. The arrogant actually walked up to the plot. Once, a Prius with a "Go Green!" bumper sticker and a Virginia Tech parking decal slammed to a halt right in front and the driver, ascetic and thinly bearded with wire glasses and an assy smile, jumped right out and over the curb, reaching for a bloom. That assy smile quickly turned to a grimace of terror and he backpedaled, tripping over the willow oak's roots and crabbing all the way back to his Ecocar before scrambling inside and fishtailing out. Lots of neighbors chuckled behind curtains that day.

Mr. Williams didn't. Mr. Williams stood on his porch and watched, like he did every day: propped against the far column, arms crossed, stance to the flowers, no expression on his face. There had never been an expression on his face in the memory of the neighborhood and never a day he did not stand on the porch, from morning light to evening dark, facing the flowers. Of course, before the flowers appeared, he didn't stand there looking at them. He merely stood there looking blankly at the street as the constant sound of Mrs. Williams' harangues drifted to him from the open windows, always open, even in winter, and Mr. Williams always on the porch, also in winter, no matter how cold. That had been his escape. With the flowers, though, there was no escape.

He was not on the porch the last time someone in the neighborhood had been stupid enough to approach the flowers. That was two Halloweens ago and it was Barty Clayton Jones. Barty was not his real first name — it was Calvin — but his slingshots and wild skateboarding and even wilder daredevil schemes had earned him the nickname. Seventeen-years-old and riding around with his friends smashing pumpkins and stealing candy bags from little kids, they came around the corner and the Accord, driven by Kelli Summers (who had been yelling "Stop it!" all night to Barty's wandering hands) came to a halt in front of the yard. "Spoooky," intoned Zeke Summers, Kelli's brother, and she said, "Stop it!" to him because she was a nervous girl, afraid of the dark, really. "Phw!" Barty snorted, "nothing to it! Show ya!" and he leaped out and ran straight for the flowers swinging a baseball bat. He passed through the first blooms and, according to Zeke, screamed once, although how he heard that with Kelli screaming, "Come back, you idiot!" over and over, no one could figure.

The police came and stood on the night porch with Mr. Williams and they all stared at the plot together as they played flashlights across it while Kelli, collapsed against her front bumper, cried, "Do something!" over and over. The police weren't stupid, though, and stayed on the porch.

About a week later, another carload of kids, friends of the former Barty, drove up and hurled three or four Molotovs at the bed. The plants caught and burned beautifully as the car sped away. Mr. Williams came out of the dark house and stood on the porch, lit by flames, no expression, and after a moment, went back inside. The plot roared in light and heat and hissed with boiling plant sap and, after ten minutes or so, burned to ash. No one called the fire department. Sunrise, the flowers were all back, as tight and blooming and wonderful as before.

Barty's family, eventually, moved away. Kelli committed suicide.

It was just acting out, those Molotovs. The kids in the car knew better but teenagers require a dramatic act to resolve their frustrations. They used to throw water balloons and rocks at Mrs. Williams when she came storming out of the house waving a cane and screeching death at them. Mr. Williams always fled around the corner of the house on those occasions and Mrs. Williams always got the kids' bikes and slammed them against the oak, bending their frames and grinning maliciously, or beating their dogs and cats to death when they had the temerity to cross her lawn and soil her roses and lilacs and pansies, so carefully planted by Mr. Williams under the watchful, hateful eye of Mrs. On occasion, she stroked him with the rake when a day lily was angled just a bit too off-center for her tastes.

She had been arrested many times, the police dragging her out of the house while she screamed and screamed, the blood from her self-inflicted wounds coursing over the porch and the lawn and the police car. Mr. Williams watched, no expression but ashen, because she would be back and then, well. No one saw Mr. Williams for a week or so after she returned from her various institutions and, when they did, he looked unwell, standing on the porch. But everyone saw Mrs. Williams every day when she was home. Every single day she stalked her yard and the sidewalk, regardless of the weather, killing squirrels or dogs, backhanding a mouthy kid, fighting the inevitable police.

But the last time the ambulance dropped her off, three days went by and she did not appear. Neither did Mr. Williams and that was wrong so someone called the police, who forced the door and, this time, took *him* away. They searched the house for many hours, guys in white overalls with plastic gloves and plastic visors and there were oversized black vans in the driveway and on the street and dog teams in and out. They found nothing and, late in the evening, they left and Mr. Williams came back.

The next morning, the flowers were there, red-bloomed and waving in the breeze, watching the street. Mr. Williams came out on the porch with a cup of coffee in his hand, froze, and stared at them without expression. Thus began his vigil.

The cops came back with bulldozers and more guys in coveralls with dogs, this time, and they dug up the bed, scattering the plants and piling the base in a hill next to the broken stalks and probing with poles and some kind of electronic devices. They took Mr. Williams away again. Three days later, they were done and they just left. Mr. Williams came back, going quietly into his house. The flowers came back, too, the next morning, as if nothing had happened. Mr. Williams resumed his vigil.

The cops didn't come back. They're not stupid.

A couple of state cops did, though. Guess they read the reports and looked at each other, went, "Come on!" and decided to bust this thing wide open. Be heroes. They harassed Mr. Williams on his porch for a while, getting nothing out of him but the non-expression, and then they walked over to the flowers. There were a couple of screams. The local cops came later and quietly towed their car away.

And so it went. You learn to live with neighborhood problems, like guys who insist on changing oil on their front lawns or kids who like to shoot BBs at your windows. You just deal. The years went by.

But then Mr. Williams stopped showing up on his porch and, after three days, there was this odor and the cops, reluctantly, went back inside. An ambulance came and paramedics took out a white-sheeted gurney with, obviously, Mr. Williams on it and the local cops decided enough was enough and they tore that house apart, taking up floor boards and taking out walls, so we heard. After three days they left, but not before pausing on the porch and staring at the flowers. They looked at each other and got in their cars and drove away.

The next morning, there was another flower bed. Six by six, adjacent to the first one, filled with beautiful tall clematis all strong and tightly bound, all blue blooms, six to seven inches across, but not facing the world. Facing the red ones.

The house stands empty. And you just deal.

*Original version in *Battered Suitcase*, Vol 1, Issue 5, October 2008,

Cistern

A truck going down the street is surprising enough these days, but a Zombie driving it?

That's just not standard Zombie behavior.

If you've ever seen any of George Romero's classics, then you already know that. It's amazing how much of Zombies George got right. I don't know if he was a genius, a prophet, or just logical. I'm guessing the latter. Creatures with soup for brains and a craving for flesh ... basic MO ain't that difficult to project.

Some things he didn't get right, though, like how it happened. In the *Night of the Living Dead* franchise, he posited a satellite crashing back to Earth and Zombies generating from the radiation. The truth was more like *28 Days Later*: a bug. Not from a lab or eeeevil military experiments, just something naturally occurring. Best explanation came from the CDC some years ago — a necrotic, animating bacteria infecting the brains of recently deceased persons. Plausible, since Zombies reproduce just like a bacterial colony.

George also didn't get the Zombie 'victim' issue quite right. When a Zombie killed you in his movies, you came back. But real Zombies don't leave enough of their kills for anything to animate. I've never seen a finger or part of an intestine suddenly come to life. You *will* turn Zombie if they bite you, as George showed, but not after a few days of weird fever and lethargy: right away, in just seconds. Scary, especially if you're standing next to the Bitee when it happens. That's pretty much how they took over the world.

See, they're fast. Very fast. Like the quick killers in *Dawn of the Dead*. You're walking along minding your own business and wham! ten or fifteen of 'em all over you, so have to get up a set of stairs. They're not very good on stairs. That's why I have a series of planks and ropes connecting the second stories of all these condos together. I can run from building to building when I don't feel like fighting.

Something else George got wrong — they'll eat each other. That's good on one hand, cuts down their numbers, but bad on the other because only the best Zombies are still around. And they'll stay around. Since the supply of tasty Lives is dwindling, the smart Zombies are increasingly turning to the dumb ones. I'd hoped they'd all eventually starve, like in the already mentioned *28 Days*, but in that movie they were just running around pissed off. Real Zombies eat well. And don't die.

They don't. Think of it, how do you kill a bacterial colony? Lysol? Tried that once and all I got was a pretty mad, but fragrant, Zombie chasing me. You have to burn them to a crisp or drop them in a vat of acid to assure a kill, so cut 'em, gut 'em and leave 'em for their friends. Or starvation. Even bacteria have to eat.

Head shots, yeah that's another one ole George messed up.

It's funny how, in the beginning, people took their cues from Romero. Even when hordes of the damn things were racing down streets sweeping up whole populations and eating them down to the toenails, a lot of folks treated them like the *Night/Dead* types (you know, the shambling blank-eyed moaners?) so went about their business like they had all day. Stupid. Long after even the dullest had given up that trope, I still ran into Lives who bought that 'head shot' thing. Shotguns and pistols are only good against Lives. Who's such a good shot they can take out the patellas of a Zombie horde running up on you at 30 mph?

Samurai sword, when you absolutely, positively have to cripple every freakin' Zombie in the room.

Love mine. It's real. Got it out of a gun shop. Man, is it sharp. I got pretty good with it by watching a bunch of Toshiro Mifune movies. Not *Kill Bill* — hokey Western concepts. Another good training film is that Robert Mitchum one, *The Yakuza*. Copy the way Takakura Ken moves and you can handle the sword pretty well.

Works like this. I'll be out during the day, which is a no-no but sometimes you have to explore possible caches in full light. Zombies don't slosh around much at night, turning into the shamblers for some reason, so we Lives pretty much live our lives by the stars. Every once in a while, though, gotta see the sun.

Funny. It's like a reverse *30 Days of Night*. With artistic license taken, of course.

Anyway, I'll be nosing around some Starbucks overlooked by previous looters (love me some fresh beans, I do) when a Zombie platoon will suddenly appear. I've got this patented move, turn like I'm running away but I'm actually spinning on my heel while drawing the sword from over my shoulder (I keep the scabbard on my back because I have orangutan arms and it's the only way to draw comfortably). I'll cut through an outstretched arm and pretty much through one leg, dropping the Zombie in the others' path, and they fall over each other like a Three Stooges routine. Then it's a matter of slicing through the pile, taking out legs and arms until they're just a bloody mass of torso, snapping at me and each other. Skedaddle before the growling and screeches attract another patrol, come back a few nights later (hoping some Lives haven't beaten me to it) and load up beans. There'll still be a few writhing torsos, but all they do is chew on their neighbors.

You'd think, with all the close contact, I'da been bitten. They've come close, but I wear anti-stick gloves and body armor and stay just out of range. I get splashed with Zombie blood quite a bit, of course, and have swallowed my share, but never suffered any effects. Odd. A bite turns you, but swallowing the blood doesn't. That drove the CDC nuts before they were overrun. A few of their Top Scientists posited it wasn't bacteria but Something Else Entirely, a new life form, a *bacrus*, a *viteria*. Whatever. I keep taking penicillin, avoid bites, go merrily on my way.

Phil thinks it's just a matter of time before we all turn, but I'm not convinced. He said my penicillin was just hardening the Something Else Entirely and eventually I'd have to eat truckloads to keep from turning. Phil is a bit of a pessimist. I laugh and offer him a couple of ampicillins to go with his Bowmore. "Get that crap away from me," but he's grinning. Phil is all right.

We Lives have a pretty robust social life, even though we're in competition. Just so many food stores in the greater metropolitan area, ya know. But, it's friendly competition and we make pains not to tread on each other's territory, disputes generally resolved through a drinking contest or an actual dual, if the disputants are just too mule-headed. We don't like doing that, because there just aren't that many of us. Fewer each week.

We meet on Friday nights at Live Music, which is Kelly's dive on the 11th floor of some building down by the river, 'Live' having a wry connotation. We sing rounds, lots of old Irish stuff like "Danny Boy" and

"Wild Rover." Pretty good time had by all. We trade gossip and will, at some point, head to the back and the Breeders. There's the pleasure aspect, of course, but also the duty to renew the species. Not that we're overly successful. We've had only two or three pregnancies come to term, and only one of those actually lived past two years. He's ten now and cute as button and turning into quite the knife man. His Mom will make an occasional appearance, to great cheers from We Happy Few. Good to hear a contralto among all those basses.

Wish we could hear more, but there just aren't a lot of women. Didn't have the strength and speed to fend off Zombies. Those that survived made their way to Breeder locations and set up shop, safe and prosperous, because we pay with food and whatever we can find. It isn't some macho chauvinism causing all this, just the natural order of things. Feminism is great in decadent, fat times, but not in a state of nature.

So no exclusive girlfriends and definitely no wives, which should mean jealousy is no longer an issue but, of course, it is. Human nature. A couple of the names on Kelly's Wall of Heroes are there because guys can't control themselves, and there's even a couple of female names for the same reason. Too bad.

And because guys can't control themselves, there's a lot of pairing among the boys. Fine. If you gotta stick it somewhere and can't wait your turn, knock yourself out.

I don't swing that way, but don't begrudge those who do. I draw the line with Zombie relations, though. Not that it happens a lot, but you hear stories. If I ever came across a Live doing a Zombie, I'd cut both of them in half. Not only is it revolting, it's species betrayal. Not going to stand for that.And I'm not going to stand for some damn Zombie driving a dump truck, either.

I watch, utterly amazed, through my peephole as the truck lumbers by. Takes me a moment to gather wits because, hey, Zombie driving a truck, but then I grab my sword and a backup tanto and head across a plank bridge in pursuit. It's full daylight and I'm armored. I'm always armored, even when sleeping, because I'm not all that convinced Zombies won't one day figure out how to get up the stairs. I mean, there's one driving a truck; who saw that coming?

The truck's not going very fast so it's not that hard staying with it until I get to the end of my complex, then I have to go downstairs and that slows me down— don't want to stumble into a pack of grazing Zombies. The street slows me down even more because Zombies are sharp sighted and, apparently, have a dog's ability to smell so I hug two-story buildings in case I gotta run. But, I manage to keep the truck in sight.

It's closed up so I have no idea what the Zombie's hauling. Probably nothing. It's just acting out some vestigial memory, just like that badass Zombie in *Land of the Dead* going out to the gas pumps every time the bell rang. I expect the truck to crash at any moment.

But it doesn't. It makes turns. Right out the city.

Which is a problem. In the 'burbs, there's a dearth of two-story buildings. No Live in his right mind lives out there. No Zombie does, either, congregating downtown hoping to snag an unwary Live and a hot meal, but that doesn't mean there aren't a few crazy Zombies tooling around. "Crazy Zombies." Ha.

So I lose sight of the truck because I'm looking for trouble, instead, but I can still hear it. You can hear everything miles away now, since traffic has died down a bit, hardy har har.

Which, of course, poses another question— how the heck did a Zombie manage to find the last functioning truck in America?

Who would *have* such a truck, stored and lovingly maintained all this time? With none of us hearing about it? No way. And a Zombie gets it started and is merrily driving it around the city?

No freakin' way.

Something else must be happening, something very very unusual and very unusual stuff is usually very bad, and I'm not one to put up with very bad things happening in my general vicinity. Being proactive is how I've stayed alive so long. A lot of the other guys hunker down behind fortifications and barricades, but that's stupid. George C. Scott said as much in *Patton*. Gonna get caught in there one day, I tell 'em. They tell me to screw off. Fine.

I'm for taking the fight to the enemy so I'll hide up on a stairwell and wait for a Zombie patrol to wander by then drop down among them, slash slash, pile of growling, snapping torsos and I'll scream real loud and another patrol will come busting in and slash slash, again, and soon there's a mountain of mad Zombie heads all trying to get me. Using their tongues to crawl, for chrissake. Makes me laugh and I leave, knowing another patrol will be there soon to eat up what's left. Cuts their numbers down and keeps them away from my hideyhole.

But if they're out driving around...

I pelt down several alleys, noting places where I can barricade a door and fight if need be, until night comes. The truck is still on the air but, after a couple of miles, I stop because, wait a minute, wait a minute...

That's not one truck anymore. That's several trucks.

A Zombie convoy?

What. The. Hell?

I haven't been out to this part of the city in a decade or more but I remember the layout. Typical industrial sector, office and factory parks surrounded by the plebes' residences, all anchored around a series of reservoirs because you gotta have water. If I recalls me geography right, there's a lovely reservoir in the direction of all that truck traffic.

What. The. Hell?

What would a bunch of trucks be doing at a lake? A bunch of trucks driven by Zombies?

No way.

Maybe somebody's figured out how to enslave Zombies and is using them as an unpaid work force for some kind of project out there, like in that old 40's flick *King of the Zombies*. Putting Zombies to good use, man, that would be revolutionary. Must check this out.

I sprint down the street, catching myself at the corner like Wile E. Coyote on one leg and jumping back inside a partially collapsed garage. Gotta be careful, even though a Zombie chain gang workin' in the coal mine has me all a-giggle. Good thing, because right about that time I catch sight of another truck moving on the street behind me.

No. not a truck. A bus. Driven by, and filled with, Zombies.

Which floors me. I have to rub my eyes a couple of times and pinch myself to make sure I'm not having some bizarre dream. The King of the Zombies has public transit, getting the Undead out to the job site like a bunch of cubicle drones?

Man, who IS this guy?

The only way to find out is follow and, fortunately, the bus is slower than the truck so I keep up. There doesn't seem to be any patrols and I move somewhat openly.

The roads here turn country pretty quick, which

means no buildings to use as shelter. Lots of woods, though, and I could climb a tree but I'm not sure if that's wise. Zombies could be like bears and just wait until I fell out from starvation. Best not to be seen. Or smelled. I hump through the brush by the side of the road, waiting for upwind breezes.

The whole time, Zombie filled buses and trucks are going by. Quite the operation, this. I throw caution to the upwinds and begin running beside the road, keeping out of sight as much as possible...

Until the smell hits me.

Gagging, I stagger back into the thick brush and clamp a hand over my nose. We Lives have quite the tolerance for rotted meat, there always being some kind of fresh kill (either Zombie or one of us) baking in the sun somewhere, but this! It's like a gas attack of decay and rot. I gasp for air at the base of a tree. The rot is so thick you can taste it.

Man, how does the King of the Zombies cope?

I crawl up some rise seeking breathable air. Back when I was in the Army, I was in really good shape, but the one thing that always did me in was the freakin' Low Crawl. I'm definitely not in as good a shape as I was back then so, a few minutes to catch my breath. Okay. Cautiously, I peer over the top.

The reservoir is below, decent sized with an earthen dam on one side and an access road all the way around, woods right up to the water's edge. Urban lake gone all to seed with remnants of picnic areas and outbuildings scattered about. Below the dam is a spillway, and I can see water pooled down there. Pretty deep, and frothy.

Frothy?

There's a line of dump trucks on the far side, one backed down a ramp and lifting its load while three or four others wait behind. A couple of Zombies emerge from the pump house, look down at the spillway, then go back inside. Moments later, the water changes flow.

They're running the pump house?

Astounding, and I shift for a better view. There's recent construction below the spillway, a makeshift cistern of some kind, but not running any wheels or dynamos or anything like that; too slow, the water just pooled there, brown and scummy. Several pipes are stuck in the lower half of it and, at each end, a Zombie stands at a turn wheel. A line of Zombies snakes back from the end of the pipes to a bunch of buses on the other side. Zombies disembark and join the queue.

I blink. What are they doing? The Zombie at the wheel turns it and brown sludge flows out, where a queued Zombie, lips around the pipe end, drinks long and deep then shuffles back up the hill to the bus. Another Zombie replaces him and the attendant Zombie turns the wheel and the guys come out of the pump house and measure progress and the dump trucks keep coming.

There ain't a Live in sight, so no King of the Zombies. This is an all-Zombie all-the-time operation, which raises a few thousand million questions, all of them beginning with, "Holy crap, what in the Sam Hill is going on?" but there's a better question:

What's in the cistern, mac?

I focus my attention on the trucks. Whatever they're dumping feeds the cistern, and given the nature of Zombie nourishment, can't be good. I watch a load slip out. Looks like a mass of brown and black dirt with lumps interspersed, say unprocessed compost. The Zombies have broken into an old sewage plant and started a hauling operation? Why didn't they all just congregate at the sewage plant and slake thirst there, why all the effort?

You think Zombies are logical?

I chuckle and that notches the tension down a bit. Okay, this IS artifact, a series of half remembered pre-Zombie tasks. Some recalled driving trucks, others recalled loading trucks. Others remember picnics so they head out on buses driven by reawakened drivers. Rote activity, twitches of a dead nervous system, just a series of coincidences making it look like there's planning and forethought.

But if it quacks like a duck ...

Uneasy, I begin another agonizing crawl just short of

the ridge top, heading towards the dump point. Need to see what's in those trucks. After about seven days and as many layers of epidermis, I'm there, panting. The trucks are using the road right below me and I peek over. Dang, the load's covered with canvas.

But the canvas is moving.

I blink. Gotta be the truck's motion but, no, the canvas is shaking and bulging and pulsing so the load is alive. What, animals? Puppies from some farm? Oh man, Zombies are just the worst, ain't they?

The truck backs down the ramp. There's a fortunate gap between tree limbs and I can look directly at the back of the truck as the Zombie driver tilts the bed and it flaps open, dumping a giant load of gnashing, screeching Zombie heads and parts into the spillway.

So, Zombies are dumping Zombies, or what's left of Zombies, into the water.

Now why in the world are they doing that?

I imagine the busses down at the cistern and the queue of Zombies slurping from the pipes and it takes a few moments because the conclusion is not only staggering, but so disgusting I feel bile rise:

Meat milkshake.

The Zombies have made a giant pool of rotted meat soup, right there in the cistern, and have set up a soup kitchen. Instead of ranging around looking for us, they've gone into mass production.

Freakin' impossible.

So startled, disgusted, terrified, whatever, I am that I make too big of a movement and a Zombie looks up, roars and points.

I am a dead man. Soon to be part of the milkshake.

There are answering roars from the truck line and the soup line and every Zombie in America will be pouring up the hillside after me. I jump up, whipping out the sword and brandishing it at the truck Zombies, who all stand in a line pointing and roaring, a lot like Donald Sutherland in that remake of *Invasion of the Body Snatchers*. "You ain't getting' me easy!" I yell and swing the sword in a threatening manner while eying the drop-off and wondering if I can scramble down, cut one of the Zombies out of a truck and drive it back home. Be nice to have a working truck.

And then the Zombies do something extraordinary:

Nothing.

After a few seconds of pointing and roaring, they get back to work. I blink. Gotta be a trick. But no, they're downright ignoring me.

What the hell?

Now I'm more peeved than anything so I stomp around, being noisy and obvious because I'd like nothing more than whittle a few of them down to stumps, but no reaction. I go back to the soup line overlook and the whole parade stops and looks at me for just a second or two and then goes back to slurping pipes. One of them actually waves.

I'm not the brightest guy, God giving me fast reactions instead of brains, but, it comes clear after a few minutes and I can't help it, I start laughing. I laugh for a good five minutes, sheathing the sword and shaking my head and even getting a couple of more friendly waves from the soup line participants.

I walk back down the hill, not even bothering to hide. The passing Zombies all react the same, a roar, a point, and then ignore. I don't get cautious until I'm back in the suburbs, but I'm not trying to avoid attack. I'm in ambush mode, something the soup line Zombies will appreciate.

I am their shepherd.

Tend to the herd, slaughtering dumb Zombies, leaving them piled in wriggling hills of meat for the smart Zombies, who'll shovel them into the back of a truck and dump them in the cistern, a continuous supply of good wholesome meatshakes. And the smart ones leave We Happy Few alone.

The benefits of symbiosis.

I hear several footfalls and growls a couple of streets over and unsheathe. Time to do my part.

*Original version in *Chivalry is Dead, An All Male Zombie Anthology*. Maydecember Publications. June 2011

The Elvish Woman

Warren met the elvish woman in some dark place, possibly woods, on a day he no longer remembered. They became lovers. Elvish women, eons ago, began taking mortal men. The limitations of mortal women provided the opportunity.

He would gasp after they made love, watching his own life dissipate on the very last breath of his passion. She would make a shape of it, some smoky thing, a heart or mythic animal like a unicorn or a griffin, and place it back on his lips. If she didn't, he would die.

She was tall and dark, but her skin was snow and her eyes deep blue, ocean currents tossing. The cascade of her hair was a black avalanche with a separate life, curling about him. He knew her by type and character from myths he had read before.

"You're very much as Tolkien described," he said one evening.

"Tolkien knew us," her voice was a harp.

"In the biblical sense?' Warren asked.

She shuddered. "Do not speak of your holy books," and she was gone.

He sometimes thought she was more ghost than elf. There were times, silhouetted against a blue sun, that she was evanescent and he knew it was a dream. In the midst of great, powerful sex, she would sometimes disappear, but he was still locked to her, still deep inside, and it seemed when she was not there she was more present than ever, and that was sheer ecstasy. Sheer terror.

"You frighten me," he told her.

"It's the nature of our two peoples," she shrugged. "You are frightened by what is different. We," she kissed him, "are entranced."

Fear and fascination, aspects of attraction, even if it was dark and wrong.

He sought her at all hours. In the morning when he readied for the day's tasks, he ran his hands across the bed, searching, and sometimes she was there and he forgot those tasks and fell into her. In the high sun, taking a rest, he walked out of his office and across streets and there would be a hint of her in some part of town he didn't know and he would run and she would be at the end of a dark street; they would fall together in shadow. In the evening, she came to him, no matter where he was.

The women, the mortal ones, watched him because the smell of her was a perfume in his wake, dead leaves and autumn, the end of things. They couldn't match it. Through lidded eyes they saw him narrowly, as someone lost to their own charms and they suspected something otherworldly. "Who is she?" asked one of the boldest. "Who?" he asked back, but not in perplexity. He genuinely wanted to know.

"Who are you?" he asked her once.

"Do you want my name?" she was fully there, naked, a shining of starlight and time to her skin, sex rising about her in waves.

"Yes."

"If you have my name, then you have my soul," she said.

"It is a dark soul."

"We are a damned people."

"I want it."

"Then you are damned," and she straddled him and his breath was gone. His eyes saw forever."*Evfnaral*," she breathed in the rhythm of their sex.

"Is that your name?" he gasped.

"No. That you will never have. It will kill me," she

panted in orgasmic joy. "It will kill you."

"Then, what is that word?"

"The transport," and she was lost in frenzy and drove deeper and his screams echoed hers.

The transport. No better word. When the smoke of her disappeared that time, it had taken him much longer to return. He was in an alley, the human world of stained concrete and overflowing dumpsters, but in a bower of laurel and mistletoe. He trembled. Mistletoe, she told him, carried the souls of wounded lovers.

He staggered back to work and sat in front of his screen, not seeing the quarterly reports. The door to his office opened and he looked up. Clarice, the office manager, sat across from him. She was a human version of the elvish woman, long dark hair and willowy limbs, blue eyes, but the eternity was not there, the seeing of dark places.

"Are you all right?" she asked.

Oh yes, he was. He told her.

"You look thin," she gave him a critical eye. "Pale. Are you sick?"

No, far from it. He told her that, too.

She cocked her head, lovely in a human way. "You're being drained," she whispered, "you're disappearing." She leaned forward, earnest concern in her eyes and Warren could see, nestled in her cleavage, a device, some intricate twisting of gold into a circlet that never ended. "You will wander dark hills and call out in agony."

"What?" Warren blinked at her but she rose and whirled the skirt about her, a cloud of obscurity, and was gone.

Warren stayed late, making the effort but he only finished half of what he should and it was dark when he stepped outside. Orion bracketed the city, and Warren wondered how he could see it, with the blinding lights of human cars and streets and stores washing away the night. The Belt gleamed at him. She said it was the belt all her race wore, and he wondered what it was like to dance on stars. A voice whispered in his ear and he turned, following the caress of it, and, hours later, he was on the edge of some leftover woods outside the highways. There she was, although she was featureless in a cloaking dark and she shifted restlessly and opened for him and he was in her arms...

Evfnaral.

The dawn came. He was alone and staggered out of the brush and cut his hand on brambles. He stumbled home.

Clarice sat on his porch. "My God," she said.

"Don't invoke your holy names," he said, and fell at his door.

When he awoke, he was in bed, naked and washed, his cuts bandaged. It was getting dark and he squinted at himself. His skin was translucent. It was taking on an elvish glow. He smiled and closed his eyes and saw dark hills rolling to the Belt. He was so alone.

Fearfully, he opened his eyes. "Hello?" he called, but no one was there. He slept.

Midnight.

He opened his eyes and she was standing at the foot of the bed, glowing, naked, so beautifully naked, a porcelain and starlight sculpture. Perfect. His breath caught and she smiled, the Belt forming about her waist and girding her sex, caressing it, exciting her. "Warren," she breathed and he threw back the sheets and she was on him, taking him, and the Belt danced and roiled through him and he screamed, "Your name!"

Her eyes burned and the smile was black and cold, "If you have it, you will wander dark hills in agony. You will scream my name over and over but you won't know its use, and I will keep you lost in those dark hills forever so none of mine will hear because they would speak it and I will be dust among the stars. Would you want that?" the coldness of her smile grew and her rhythm frenzied and she grasped him and he was centered, centered.

"No! No!" he gasped but, oh, everything he was, his soul, was draining out of him and into her and there was nothing but the way she offered and she seized and caressed and sank on him and he roared, as his entire essence roared into her, "Yes! Tell me!"

She leaned back still containing him, her face twisted in fury, her hair now white and powerful and her eyes black light and cold stars, "Then, have it!" and she screamed, "Thulwyn!"

"Thulwyn!" he screamed back and saw, before him, black hills spinning upwards, black lonely hills of eternity where regrets and loss stalked the valleys, and he choked in fear ...

as another voice said quietly, "Thulwyn."

She leaped off him, straight up, suspended in the air and clawing at her face. He was ripped back from the surface of the black hills and fell hard into his bed, staring up at the elvish woman, who spun, her teeth gnashing and her tongue going bloody from it.

Clarice stood at the end of the bed. "Thulwyn," she said again, the gold device clasped in her hand.

Thulwyn bellowed a horror of a voice, her arms extending into claws and she slashed at Clarice, who fell before the force of it. But it was too late. Thulwyn turned, staring mournfully at Warren. "I am undone," she said, and slowly sank to the floor, her eyes the currents of the ocean, her skin the glow of starlight, her hair black again, like the black hills of agony.

"No!" Warren cried and leaped from the bed, falling on the pile of stardust and frantically scrambled through it. At the bottom was a sprig of mistletoe.

He buried Clarice in those same leftover woods.

There were queries but they soon died. She had been an odd woman.

Warren became an odd man, the air about him black and mournful, and he made others shudder. At night, he walked the dark hills of human buildings, loss and despair ever present in the alleys he passed, cupping a sprig of mistletoe. And he whispered her name.

*Original version in *Midnight in Hell,* Sep 2009

The Trumpet Inside the Warehouse

Your Worships, I gives testimony on these recent, sad events with great sorrow, great sorrow. It is my feeling that much of what happened is my own fault; iff'n I'd been more attentive, more keen, then could I've said or done something that woulda stopped it all. I mourn these two fine men, especially Mr. Otten. I think a little more brightness on my part coulda prevented his terrible death.

I have your repeated assurances that I am not to blame. I am most appreciative of Your Worships' sympathy and support, but I was in a position, very early on, to realize the mis-intent of Sir Belyard. Had I done a better job connecting the odd goings-ons about the Cousen Lane warehouse with his final purpose, well, I am greatly pained by it, greatly pained.

You see, sirs, I ha' beadled the All Hallows parish for almost thirty years now and I kin the smallest thing out of sorts there like a tiny splinter itching me palm. I spy a new buzzman like he dressed in mufti and wore a sign, and I am very, very proud of the ones I've run off and the ones I've caged. It's not an easy labor, I tell you sirs, to keep our streets safe and our people unmolested.

So when I sees the young man carrying the shiny brass trumpet, I was intrigued. I was standing on the corner off Cousen's, idling a bit as is my wont at the midday, when things have slowed considerably, sirs. I was not completely at ease for I was speaking with a Metropolitan, a good Peeler I have had the pleasure of working the waterfront with before, sirs, and indeed it was he, Cardle being his name, who pointed out the young man. Now I am not a music hater, sirs, and it was not the trumpet that raised suspicion but the person who had his hands wrapped about it. He was a street wretch named Pennington that both Cardle and I pinched on several occasions afore. He was a cut purse, sirs, and a snatcher, one familiar to you gentleman. Golden tongued, he avoided transport and the gallows three times to me knowledge, sirs. A wily one, a wily one. I do not mean to impugn your honor's acumen in letting him go previously, but whenever he was about, something no good was about, also.

So Cardle reaches out and grabs the boy by the arm as he walks by us, bold as you please, as if we were no ones to account. "Here now!" Cardle says, "what have you gone and lifted this time, Penny?"

"Off me, copper! I'm a law-abiding citizen!" he yells to us both and, naturally, we are taken up by much laughing over that.

"Why, so the Saints have marched on the Vatican, have they? A monkey's got the throne, and you're law abiding!" I says back and I have to say that is the way of us out there, sirs, this rude talk among the cons and cuts; it is the only language they speak and I do not mean to offend. Anyways, me and Cardle are both laughin' now rather hardy and we have the boy darbied and he screechin' and flailin' at us the whole time about mindin' his own business and doing some work for a 'gennlmen' and gone legit and we's just harassin' good innocent folk and it's startin' to get a bit testy and I am lowerin' me staff when he says, "I can prove it, I can prove it!"

"Then prove it, ya whelp," Cardle says to him.

"I can, I tells ya!" he says, "You just take me over to the 3rd Alley warehouse and see Sir Belyard. He'll tell ya he sent me to fetch the trumpet."

"Sir Belyard, is it?" I says, "A baronet? More likely a

gypsy king!" And Cardle and I are laughin' some more.

"Just take me there," Pennington cries, so we did, we marched him straight over between us, kicking him forward the whole time and tellin' him how much worse it's gonna be for his lyin'.

Well, sirs, we get there and there is some comin's and goin's as you'd expect but not so much at the 3rd Alley, because that's a night port and the packets are still down river and I was half expectin' part of Penny's gang to be laying there for us. I don't mind tellin' you gentleman that I fancy a bit of the staff work from time to time. I know the Peelers aren't much for it and prefer to court and judge, but we beadles have our own traditions. I'd just as well break a few heads and leave them bleedin' in the street and save the Crown a crown or two. I see some of Your Worships are in some agreement, so you can then know I was ready for it. Cardle had his stick and he was ready, too, but it wasn't a gang that came out to meet us, no sirs.

It was a gentleman, sirs, at least that's how he appeared to us then. We know different now, but you wouldna thought otherwise, had you been there. He was dressed in all white, sirs, coat and pants, with a ruffled shirt and a black cummerbund and cravat to set off the whiteness, even a red kerchief peeking so lightly out of the coat pocket. He had on a white topper, too, sirs, and was carrying a silver wolf's head cane. He was a tall man, sirs, a good head above me, and I stand three cubit, and a dark one, seemed a lot of the French in him but with real blue eyes, Saxon like. A strong one, too, I could tell. Something about the set of his shoulders spoke trouble and I hefted me staff as he walked up. I thought at first the set came from soldiering, but we know now what it was.

"Mr. Pennington," he addresses our prisoner, fine spoken tones, too, "what seems to be the trouble?"

I cannot tell you, sirs, how astonied I was at these words. It seemed Pennington was right and he began looking very satisfied while both Cardle and I shared a rather different expression.

"I'll tell ya the trouble, Sir Belyard, these two nithings ..."

And here, sirs, Cardle cuffed Penny good, as he deserved for that and I was thinking of adding a bit of staff work when the gentlemen steps between me and my intended target. "Here, officers," he says, "there's no call for that. This young man works for me."

"For you, sir?" I asks, "doing what?"

"He was to fetch a trumpet from the brokers off Cousen's, where I presume you officers saw him?" Sir Belyard was calm and refined, but, still, sirs, there was a thing in his voice that begged at me right off. I can say now what it is, but then it was that splinter in me palm. Something was not right and the presence of a nice suit is no surety against wrongdoing, so I kept my staff loose and aimed because I was not so sure 'tweren't needed.

"And why would you be using the likes of him?" Cardle asked with his stick ready, too, and it eased me quite a bit to see we was sharin' a thought.

Sir Belyard must have seen that, too, because he smoothed back and put on a most disarming smile, "I understand your suspicions. But I have come here to give unfortunates like Mr. Pennington," and he gestures at the wharf rat, "an opportunity for a better, productive life."

"This thief?" Cardle again, which elicited a yelp from Pennington about slander. "How ya proposin' that?" So Sir Belyard leaned into us, conspiracy like. "Can you officers keep a secret?" he asked.

Now me and Cardle are not blabbermouths and, when it has nothing to do with the public safety or good order, we are not ones to be tellin' business of others, what gentleman is visitin' what discreet location, what Lord has trouble walkin' out of his Club, what Lady is steppin' out of a carriage where she shouldn't be, sirs. But to be asked straight like that were a warnin' to us both of something untoward and we both looked at Sir Belyard, ready to brain him for anything unsavory. So we were both taken back a bit when he whispered one word to us, "Music."

"Music, sir?" I was a bit bewildered.

"Yes, Beadle. Music, the universal language. Soothes the savage breast, as Mr. Congreve so charmingly put it. I am forming a band, officers."

"Band, sir?"

"Yes, officers," he says back, "a band these unfortunate street gypsies will play in and so make their way back into society's good graces," and he looked at us with a truly satisfied smile.

Cardle and I both took to guffawing over this, the idea of Pennington or Ward Lucy or Gin Bucket Jack tootin' and a blowin' to the delight of an audience. Most mirthful. Pennington and Sir Belyard stood there and watched us and took no offense, which I should have seen at the time that they, the authors of this story, had no more faith in it than we. But I supposed then that Sir Belyard was one of those reformers who, God Bless their simple spirits, are convinced some kind of activity is all the criminals and cheats and bad hearts of the world need to reform.

"I didn't say it would be easy," he allowed to us with a smile, which made us both laugh all the more. "Indeed, officers, it will take much time and practice, which is why I have acquired this warehouse," and he points back at it, "and why I have asked Mr. Pennington to bring the trumpet. You see, officers, it is not my wish to offend the public while my new band begins its long, torturous journey into the realm of Aoede, so we will practice in here." And he slapped the high wooden wall. "I asked for the trumpet to see if it could be heard in the street."

He made a gesture at Mr. Pennington, who shook off Cardle, gathered up the trumpet, smirked at us and went inside, the double door coming to a ponderous close behind him. We stood there, me and Cardle, pop-eyed at the whole idea while Sir Belyard stood facin' us with a sincere grin. About a few minutes of that, and Pennington comes back, lookin' a bit red. "Well?" he asks all of us.

Sir Belyard's grin becomes a triumph and he holds his hands out, "Not a sound. Perfect!" I thought he would clap hands like some school girl and it was odd, most odd, sirs. Pennington beamed around but there was the splinter diggin' at me. "How do we know you played it?" I asked him.

Pennington took himself a breath the likes of a man bigger than him to start some kind of screechin' when Sir Belyard raised a hand. "Fair question, Beadle," and he turned to Pennington. "Why don't you take the Beadle inside and blow the horn and the Metro man and I will wait out here to listen," and he swept his hat off at the idea and there was nothin' for me to do then but follow.

It was a most peculiar place to be startin' a band, was my first thought. Dark inside, too dark, with no windows, not even high ones for a breath of air and the planking particularly thick, doubled, I was thinking and I was wondering what the need for such strength. I know the 'house, of course, seeing it part of my parish for these years, sirs, but never been inside. It seemed to me that whoever commissioned it, before my time, sirs, was thinkin' of precious cargoes, jewels or silks or some such, because the 'house was a fortress. The breakers would have a whole night's work to get in, and there's not enough ambition in the whole lot to see it through. Good place if you want to muffle the sounds of your new band, I was thinkin', but a dreadfully stuffy place for them to do it.

Pennington took me to the main room, which was as dreary and airless as the passage, and I was a bit startled by the size of it. Very tall ceilings with many beams crisscrossed and supporting each other, allowing many weights to be dropped there. Pennington began a blatting and twirping on that trumpet enough to call Lucifer's own sons to see what the bellowing was about. I clapped my hands over my ears, almost losing my staff and endured about a minute of it before I yelled, "Enough of this!" and marched myself outside.

Cardle and Sir Belyard looked at me and, no doubt, sirs, no doubt, could tell from my disturbed air that Pennington had indeed blown the trumpet and called the dead. Sir Belyard smiled at us both and almost went into that girlish dance again. "It works, it works!" he cried happily and begins to jig Pennington around. Cardle and I had enough of this and we took ourselves off, but not without some rude words from Pennington that Sir Belyard made no attempt to smother.

Sirs, as you have told me, Sir Belyard being an odd one was not out of line for some long blooded families that have wearied themselves with intrigues and dissipations of the kind we usually do not mention. Such families are entitled to their eccentrics and their half-mads, and what I had seen of Sir Belyard certainly convinced me he was a bit of both. But he bothered me still, and I don't just say that because of what we now know. That he was a large hearted do- gooder bent on reformin' the criminal mind I was sure, but I was equally sure he had a shade of it himself.

So I made it a point to take the extra-long stroll when I was warding to see what hijinks was stirring about that alley. I full expected, at best, to find Pennington's gang takin' vantage of Sir Belyard's innocence and usin' the warehouse for new kinds of mischief. At worse, they'd be smugglers plying black trade between Irishers and Dutchmen, with Sir Belyard overseein' the lot. One, t'other, or somethin' between.

But I did not see that. I did not see much of anything, sirs, and I was right puzzled by it. Just in the normal course of commerce, you'd expect such a stout 'house to be busy. But, sirs, I saw the place dark and deserted more than I saw anything. After a while, I fell into a complacency about it, shortin' my strolls as new events vied for me attentions.

I could be forgiven for that, I s'pose. Then I would have a clear conscience with Your Worships about what I should have known and when. Exceptin', sirs, there were two strange events in those weeks that shoulda, by themselves, roused me to a greater concern. I shoulda let others bear me out; maybe they'd see what I couldn't. But I did not, and I remain in apology for that, sirs, in apology.

The first of these was the delivery of chains and buckles to the warehouse during the dark of new moon past. I had attended to a body nearby and was, just by accident, makin' my way through the alley. I was interested when a wagon pulled up, and made more so when I saw the carters strugglin' with the boxes. When they dropped one and I hear the clinkin' of metal, I thought they was haulin' coinage of some kind, maybe from the Dutchers, and we had a bogus set up inside. So I made way, staff ready to give a headin' to them all. "Here now!" I called, "wot's all this?"

Can you, sirs, imagine much of my startlement when one of the carters turns to me and is Sir Belyard himself? He was done up in dungarees and the worker's jacket, a brim hat, too, and him as dirty as the wharfers he had with him. I was feelin' the need to admonish the gentleman about his get-up, so unseemly, when he says, "Beadle, I am most surprised to see you."

"I am certain that you are, sir," I says back, "as astonied as I, you."

He looks down at himself and laughs. "Have to indulge me, Beadle," he says, "I am an idle-handed man and sometimes feel the need to do some true work. Sometimes, rather than ordering ones about, I like to be ordered."

That seemed in keeping with my opinion of the man but still did not shake my concerns about the heavy, coin clinking boxes, so I step up, bold as I can, and says, "I am wondering of your cargo, Sir Belyard."

"This?" and he sweeps his hands so prettily at the long boxes. "These are for the band."

And I looks and they are the chains I have already mentioned, sirs, big, long chains, naval types, not for anchors or anythin's like that but for masts and such. "And why would a band need chains?" I ask.

"You are a suspicious one, Beadle," he laughs and makes it like some kind of joke but he is irritated with me, I can tell, and so the carters and they start a-mutterin' among themselves and I heft my staff at them to shut them up. "No need for that, boys," he says to them and gives me this smile that, I'm telling you sirs, was that of Eden's Adder. "Some instruments require hanging, Beadle."

"Hanging?" I ask him because I had never heard such a thing. "Yes, Beadle," he says, "the larger instruments, the bell cornets, for one, have to be hauled up to drain and tune."

I am sufficient in this world, sirs, to know there are things I do not know, especially in these astounding times where men read the lives of others through head-bumps and Colt puts out a revolving pistol. So when a gentleman tells me of musical techniques unknown to me, I am one to take him at his word, sirs, his word. That it was a night delivery I considered odd, but I did not question that either, sirs, accustomed by now to Sir Belyard's strangeness.

The next event was a comment made to me when I was tearing after a gander fleeing down one of the rows. I fairly yanked him off his feet and got his perfume thrown in my face for the trouble, so I stroked him once to keep him quiet while I wiped my eyes. "Todd," he gasps at me, holding his bloody mouth, "you'll be payin' the Todd!" And I was dumbstruck, sirs, dumbstruck, because he's callin' at me the bogeyman. I almost fell to laughin' at it, such a boyish, childish thing to say, but something to expect from that ilk. 'Cept the look on his face was not of the soft sorrowful types they are, but a man angry, a man seekin' to do me violence.

I shook him then and says, "Stupid talk! What am I,

then, just a poppet?"

And he grabbed at me and he grinned real evil and he says, "He's back! And he's paying back!" So I stroked him then as a damn fool and hauled him off to Newgate. But the words stayed with me, sirs.

These were the settin's when the first trouble began, sirs, the first with Mr. Otten. A tribute to the beadling, sirs, that one, and a man I most respected, most respected. I knew well his role in the St. Dunstan's horror those thirty years ago and learned some of the skills of it from his own mouth. And I shoulda connected it, sirs, especially after the gander's strange sayin'. But I had not the brain for it.

I was on the street talking with some of the church wardens, sirs, when Cardle comes running to me all out of breath. "Beadle!" he calls, "Alarm, sir! Some ruffians have stolen Mr. Otten right out of his home, sir!" I was completely astonied, as were my wardens and we scattered quickly enough in hopes to intercept such godless men, attacking an old and health-broken gentleman like that. The very idea, sirs, made me ill and quite determined to run them down, but we were not lucky in that regard, sirs, as you well know. And I am heartbroken about it.

In that excitement, sirs, the second trouble seemed less important and I did not give it the thorough consideration it demanded. A respectable man like Mr.

Otten spirited out of hearth seemed to me much more heinous than the young man, Lord Burton, set upon in his carriage and carried away so roughly. When I first heard of it, we was still in the pursuit of Otten's malefactors and I dismissed it, I readily admit, as the just desserts young Lords get when they spend too much time in the dives and among the gamblin' pits. I did not think the two related. I did not see how they could be.

I have read the recent accounts, sirs, where some old Bow Streeters claim they connected poor Mr. Otten and Lord Burton to St. Dunstan's right away. But I say, here and now, sirs, that those men are shameful. If they truly saw it, my Lords, then why did they not speak up? At the very least, they could have spoken to me. They know me as a man willin' to hear and learn from others and I hold the Bow Streeters in good regards, sir, even as so many these days don't, which I think wrongheaded. These sudden claims of a greater insight than those of us working at the time is all after the fact and all self-serving, in my opinion, sirs.

As it were, I was most heartsick over the grabbing of Mr. Otten, and I had no rest those four days, scouring the parish seeking out even the slimmest of clues. I know we was somewhat out the bounds, but it seems more than most fruits of most crimes end up in my parts and, if Mr. Otten himself did not appear, there was still a very good chance one of his violators would. It was for that reason I was about the end of Cousen Lane when I saw a crowd gathered and heard a few of the tarts shrieking.

"Give way!" I hollered at the slackers and drunks and was pushin' them apart with my staff. Their expressions started out eager and curious, but, as I made my way forward, became concern and then fright and revulsion. My progress got harder because the frightened ones was turnin' straight into me, prompting a couple of strokes to clear 'em off. By that way, I suddenly found myself up front, with the ones there making a concerted effort to get round the ones pressin' behind.

At first I was not sure what I was seein'. The fog was in thick that night and the gas lamps was not makin' much against it. There were some torches about but they had a flickerin' to them so it took me a moment to realize that something was crawling towards me. I thought it was a badly injured dog at first, but it was bigger than that, so I had a wild thought that a pig had been run over, lost its legs and was flopping around on its belly. But then someone brought some lanterns and some light fell as it crawled up to me feet and I sees it was a man. Or what was left of a man.

He was all red, bloody red, that I saw right away, and I wondered at what kind a beatin' could make a man so pulped. He was leavin' a trail of himself behind,

I could see, and something else that made a clinking sound. And when I looked to see what that was I noted his feet were missin'. Here was a man had been in a right bad accident, and I stooped down to him and saw his hands was missin' too. He was reachin' with his stumps at me ankle and wheezin, "Help me, help me."

"We got you now," I says to him, "we'll get you off to the hospital here right quick," though I figured he was dead and was sayin' that just for the comfort.

And as I reached down, some stalwart lowered a lamp for better view and I see a sight that made me want to shriek as loud as the doxies were doin'. For the man had no skin, from the top of his head down to his missin' foot, not a shred, save for one patch 'round his right eye, lookin' like a fleshy stamp on a red mass of worms, sirs. I do not mean to sound so frightful, sirs, but it was the most horrid sight, most horrid, and I cannot rid my mind of it. It struck me dumb and then the smell of his blood washed over me and I could not help but stand up affright. "Help me," the pathetic thing wheezed again and stumped at me boot, but I jumped back, I am ashamed to say. I was filled with a loathin' and a revulsion, and just stood there starin' as he begged and begged me. I could not wonder at the pain he felt, his skin off and the nerves all exposed and rubbed on the cobblestone, having crawled as far as he did and no one to see in the fog or lend a hand or, those that did, runnin' away until he got to our fairly traveled street. I knew there was no doctor on earth could save him, no chance he had of living, but I could not bring myself to lend him a comfortin' hand or a cool drop of water. I leaned back into the crowd behind me.

It was most un-Christian, and I think the shame of that brought me about and I sees it is my duty to help this man, no matter how horrible the sight. So I bents down to him and his stump lands 'gainst my leg and I am chilled by the bloody touch of his worm-lookin' flesh but this is a sufferin' man, I tells myself, and I may be the last he can speak to. "Lad," I says, "what has happened to ye?" He starts wheezing at me then, his voice hard to understand, so hoarse and cracked and I realizes it must be from all the screamin' he did. The mob starts pushin' hard and agitating to see and I stand up and I roar at them to be still and push them with the staff, and I bend back down, "How did this happen, lad?" I ask him again.

It's apparent he is dyin', and even if Dr. Bobbie Todd himself came upon us, he couldna saved him. "Todd," he croaks at me, "Todd." I shake my head 'cause I am thinkin' he's thinkin' of the good doctor as I am. "Lad, he cannot help you now. Tell me what..." and here there's some strength comes through him and he stumps me hard about the boot and croaks the loudest he can, "Todd! Sweeney Todd!" and his strength goes out and he gurgles and dies there, sirs.

I am struck by that, sirs, struck, and, in that moment, what the gander said to me comes back. Here a ripped man, dyin' in the worst kind of agony, invokes the devil himself and I am, I am not ashamed to tell you, sirs, frightened to almost my own end. Sweeney Todd hanged, these thirty years now, and I have a man here sayin' the Demon himself did this! Was I facin' a vengeful ghost? You would ask yourself the same nonsense, sirs, had you seen the man and heard his terrible raspin'. At this point the light fell brighter and I looked at where his feet and hands shoulda been and sees half buckles and catch chains clinging to the stumps. It occurs to me the wretch escaped by worrying his limbs off, leaving them behind. And then I realized where I'd seen those buckles before.

"Quick!" I turns to the stalwart with the lamp, "fetch the Peelers, Cardle if you can find 'im, and have 'em to the 3rd Alley Warehouse!" and he nods and heads off and I hope you sirs will reward him for his quick mind and quick feet because, by the time I got to the warehouse door, Cardle and two of his bully boys were with me. We pounds and pounds and shouts, but there is no answer so we takes ourselfs into rammin' the door and, between the three of us, make a dent enough I can force apart with the staff. Cardle reaches in and finds the latches and we run in.

The first thing I notices is the smell, like slow drippin of blood over some days, sirs, like at the butcheries. The second I notice is the sound, sirs, a low moanin', the cryin's of someone in great pain and great loss. It makes the hair on all our heads stands and we looks at each other and Cardle points and I can see a light up where the big room was. I lead that way and there we see the most horrible sight. Another skinned man is hanging from the ceilin', his feet buckled and chained and him stretched out. His skin is lyin' at his feet. He's got one patch of skin over his left eye, and it occurs to me the skinner did that so the man could watch what was happenin'. There's another set of bloody chains on the ground with a foot still in one buckle. And there stood Pennington, with a great knife in his hand, a working at the man's belly to silence him before the escapee raised the alarm.

"Whoreson!" I yell, which startles Penny into droppin' the knife. He did not hear us enter, which was the warehouse's disadvantage, sirs. He rushes off to the rear but I am as fast as Hermes' Feet when aroused, sirs, and I reach him and stroke him hard across the top of his head, fellin' him. I stroke him some more as he lays there, layin his skull open and spilling some brain, breakin' ribs in, too, sirs. I hope you can understand my rage, sirs, because I recognized the hanging man that Pennington was skewering as Mr. Otten himself, and seein' such a revered old beadle so handled brought it on me.

I turned to watch Cardle tryin' to get the now dead Mr. Otten down from that ghastly suspension, when I hears Pennington cough and laugh, actually laugh. I turns, then, sirs, to his bloody heap on the floor, angry I hadn't done him and I reaches down and I shakes him, sirs, shakes him as hard as I can to end his worthless life. "What for, Penny? What for?" I yells.

"Paid," he coughs blood at me.

"What's paid, Penny, what?"

"Blood debt," he coughs more at me.

"Whose blood debt?"

And he looks at me and the lights in his eyes are going out and he smiles, sirs, and with his last breath, says, "Todd's."

There are better witnesses, sirs, for the hunt for Sir Belyard and they can tell you how completely he disappeared, save for that one set of white clothes that we now know he murdered a gentleman in the south for. As to where he came from and where he has gone, I cannot offer anything more than what you already know. I can, though, offer an opinion as to what Pennington said.

Sirs, I do not for one moment believe that Sir Belyard was the risen Demon, bent on a vengeance past the grave. I believe, sirs, that he is something worse. He is the vanguard of somethin' evil, sirs, somethin's you all fear, as the decent men you are. We have all been seein' and commentin' on these changin' times, when it seems the sense of common decency is fleeing us. We are all seeing these new philosophies, the levelin', the disrespect.

It is from these modern thoughts that Sir Belyard arises, sirs. Imagine a man who rejects all of decency, who holds all that is good in the greatest of contempts, who sneers at his betters and is consumed with the jealousy and anarchy that seems to be seizin' the lowest classes these days. A man like that could take a Demon like Todd and swear an allegiance to him, could take to thinkin' that the Todd was unjustly done, sir, that he was a hero. And a man like that could plan a revenge in the Todd's name, calling himself after the Bell Yard, where his idols served up the human meat pies, strippin' down to nerve Lord Burton, the son of the man who prosecuted Todd, and Mr. Otten, the very beadle who discovered the remains of Todd's victims beneath St. Dunstan's. A monstrous and evil deed to us, sirs, but an honorable deed to him.

I see that I have shocked you with this and you are wont to tell me that such is preposterous, that Belyard was just a madman. But, sirs, he was not. From my years of seein' the great evils that men can do, I can tell you that only a man driven by the greatest of hates could have planned and executed something so ghastly. That man was burnin' in his soul for many years, sirs, bent on revengin' an ill-usage he fancied, and only a man with clear thinkin' 'bout him coulda done so. A smart one, sirs, one that could have used his considerable gifts of brain and brawn to better himself but no, he uses it for this.

And I fears, sirs, he is just the beginnin'.

*Original in Ezine *Bewildering Stories,* issue 283, Mar 24, 2008.

King of the Bears

I was fly fishing along Gunsight Pass in the Bridger Wilderness, a place unbothered. It's why I go there. Rough country, discouraging day packers and weekend warriors. Lakes rise with the Continental Divide here and I follow their runoff to the Gros and Green Rivers, depending on which side of the continent I feel like strolling.

I found it five years ago, after the third divorce and fourth board ouster. I was really, really tired of people and wanted some place bereft of them. At the end of a two-week aimless wander, I left the S600 at the Gannet Peak trailhead and walked my loafered and Prada'd self up to where the rivers slid away from each other at the top of Gunsight. "Wow," I said. Since then, the S600 has given way to an S10 and the Pradas to army surplus, while I'm only part time on some board or other and no more wives. Better.

It was afternoon. Sunlight here takes on mystic character and I was satisfied, truly satisfied. I had two cutthroats and one brook, dinner guaranteed (I am not a catch-and-release wuss), had lost only one nymph, was two beers down (the runoff keeps 'em cold), and knew this was the best of life. No demands, no deadlines, no longer Master of the Universe, true, but master of myself. Happy? No, that's impossible, but content, yes, and I reached into a pocket for a pemmican stick, smiling, when I heard the grunt.

I knew what it was. I'd encountered bears here before, blacks mostly, which are curious and playful but generally leave you alone, and browns, which are morose and staring and won't leave you alone. It came from my four o'clock and I stole a look, ready to jump in the water and ride the freezing current to safety, if necessary. At first I couldn't see it — the lodgepole was pretty thick, with layers of wild currant lacing the trees together. But then, the entire mountain moved and I turned full around to see what the heck was that, landslide?

No such luck. Grizzly. Silvertip. Standing up, leaning against an aspen for support and staring at me.

It was absolutely the biggest creature on the face of this earth, that judgment not due to sudden shock. It simply was. At least ten feet tall, at least two tons, huge for a bear, colossal for a grizzly. Grayer than most, so old, with great scarring across its belly and shoulders, so a fighter. Eyes that burned like coal and teeth bore back in savagery and claws gripping through a two-inch branch, so mad.

I was a dead man.

Which was a liberating thought. If you know you haven't a chance in hell, you'll try anything, instead of standing there, paralyzed, and hoping the King Kong of bears will just go away. As it dropped to all fours, I dropped the pole, unholstered the can of bear mace and let him have it.

Jim Bridger, whose name graces this area, would have leveled his Sharps .50 and, with steady aim and fearless concentration, placed a giant round through the brain pan or heart of the fur locomotive roaring down on me. Most of the other mountain men would do that, too. But modern life has made steady aim and fearless concentration rare, and the requisite Sharps rarer, so, bear mace. Damned effective, as I've proven to myself on at least three prior occasions.

Accuracy is not necessary and the stream caught the charging bear in the chest. It's something to watch a bear caught in the spray. It'll actually knock one unconscious — I've seen that — at the minimum, stop 'em cold. A bear's skull is nothing but a giant, hyper scent receptor so, imagine, hot peppers shoved up its nose at 120 feet per second. Gives it pause.

Did here, too, but not like I expected. The bear collapsed into itself, just the oddest sight, a writhing and screaming fur mountain twisting and tearing within the span of its bulk no more than fifteen yards away. Power like that can start tornadoes and I leaped out of the way as the bear dervish whirled to the edge of the run-off. The bear stood up straight, roaring the end of the world, its paws clamped hard across its eyes and snout, and then fell, like a downed redwood, face first into the water.

I thought it was dead. Or in a coma. I stood there dumbfounded, watching the shuddering bear as the counter-wake from its fall washed back over the top of its head. "No one's going to believe this," I said and fished around in a pocket for my phone to snap a picture. I was so busy getting set that I didn't really notice what was going on until I got the picture focused and framed, and, even then, it took a moment to register.

The bear was washing the spray off its face.

"No way," I said, blinking at the picture, and I looked up to see if this was a trick of the light. It wasn't. "No freakin' way," I said again, wondering what I should do, take more pictures or get out of there.

Should have got out of there.

The bear rose straight up, rearing back on its legs and turning, the river falling off its face and down its chest. It looked at me.

Imagine your scariest beast-type nightmare — Wolfman, the Hulk, the T-Rex from *Jurassic Park* — standing twenty feet away, face burned red from pepper, eyes squinted so hard with hate they're almost gone, gigantic spiked paws out and turned towards you, the massive hump draped across its shoulders, fangs a foot long bared at your head. Multiply that by ten. Then add the most apocalyptic, spine shattering animal roar of rage and revenge, and you'll have some approximation of what I faced.

I ran. I ran very fast.

You cannot outrun a bear. There's no way. And forget all those stories about bears unable to run up or down slopes — yes they can, especially when they are very pissed off. That's why "they" (you know who "they" are) say not to run but fall down and play dead. Bears only attack people because we startle them or somehow present a threat. You fall down, no longer a threat, bear goes away after batting you around a bit. But this bear was fully intent on evisceration and my falling down would just make his job easier, so I pelted up the slope, bee-lining for the thickest part of the trees. I couldn't outrun him, but I maybe could out-slip him.

I ducked under three or four aspens growing close

together, the bear's paws slapping the ground behind me. He hit the trees hard, roaring, and smashed them out of his way but was slowed and I ducked under another close growth, the bear in pursuit, and getting madder with each new tree he had to break through. Good. If he gets frustrated enough, he'll quit. I hoped.

My path took a zigzag up the ridge, from stand to stand, the bear crashing into each one like a souped-up bulldozer. But the distance between us grew so I pumped my elbows and knees and blew through the thickest stands I could find, ripping my shirt and chest across blackberry thickets, taking half of them with me in my terror. Someone watching from a distance would see a vine-covered, bleeding crazy man bursting through undergrowth while a limb-festooned bear monster roared after him.

The angle increased, making a harder climb, but that was good; a few more stands, and the worn-out bear would take solace in scaring the bejesus out of me and go away. That is, if the stitch in my side and the fire in my lungs didn't drop me first. I spurred, crashing through ... into a wide-open glade, with far too much real estate between the next stand and me.

There was a roar of triumph and I turned and saw the most terrifying of what had been several terrifying sights so far: the bear was standing − yes, actually standing − about ten yards behind, his giant paws thrusting aspens away from him on either side, head bent and just roaring. My legs quivered into jelly and I collapsed on the ground, staring in horror, the bear's breath washing over me like a carrion breeze. I was dead. I could not get away. I think I said "Mama" a couple of times as I waited for it to fall on me.

But it didn't. It stood, regarded me, and then, I swear, it smiled.

So maybe you'd say it was a snarl and that I imagined it. No. It was a smile, of victory, of contempt, of sheer disdain. The chills that surged up my back confirmed it, and also gave me a sense of sheer disbelief. Just who the hell did this bear think he was? I looked straight at the sneering face. "Fuck you," I said.

The bear dropped into the glade, his eyes murderous and rumbled towards me. "And screw you!" I yelled and leaped to my feet like a gymnast and turned and ran towards the other side of the glade straight for a twenty-foot birch sitting right at the edge.

The angle gave me the advantage in the start, but the bear would be up to speed in seconds so I rushed the birch, wrapped my arms and legs around it and shinnied up to the first level of branches like Cheetah escaping lions.

They say don't climb a tree. They're right; bears climb better than you and all you're doing is providing a great opportunity for them to grab your legs and haul you down for a mid-day snack. But I gambled on two things; the birch was flimsy and the bear was gigantic, so it'd be too heavy to climb up. That is, if I could get out of its reach.

Which was an issue. I grabbed the first set of branches and felt hot breath on my shoulder and looked and the bear's face was just a foot or two away. I yelled (no, screamed. Like a little girl) and swung around the tree as a paw the size of a boulder destroyed the branch I had just been on, shrapneling the bark. I yanked myself up as the bear screamed like a banshee, not a little girl, and came around that side of the tree. Terror can make you an athlete and I scrambled up in record time, giant blurs of claw racking past my head. But I made it, at the top, out of reach.

But not out of danger. I still had four more days on the permit and no one would come looking until the sixth day, and spending a week in a tree — no water, no food — while a demon bear stalked below ... well, you can see the problem. I clung to the thin trunk while taking in giant gasps of air. Had to get my wind back and shout for help, hope some passing Ranger would hear and drive it off.

The bear, eyes red and insane, put a giant paw on the trunk, testing it. Yes, Bruin, won't hold you, and I breathed relief. The bear backed out of the limb cover and sat down, staring me in the eye. I stared back, which you're not supposed to do with any animal, too much of a challenge, but this bear was off script anyway. "What the HELL do you want?" I shouted at him and he snarled meaner, if that was possible, and looked over his shoulder. I followed his glance and gasped.

There were other bears.

Not just one or two, not his (or her) cubs, but seven or eight that I could see, suggestions of more back in the stand. All full grown. And not just grizzlies. Browns, blacks, Kodiaks. Even, I swear, a polar. I almost crapped myself. The bear looked back at me, meaningfully. And I knew what he wanted.

To vanquish the enemy.

The bear lurched off his seat and hit the base of the tree like Brian Urlacher. The birch shook and almost dislodged me and he reared back and hit it again. And again. The tree canted and I heard a splintering from the base and it was either going to fall over or snap under this treatment. If it snapped, I landed at the bear's feet and he and his friends would have barbecue. Falling, it went through the trees, which was my only chance.

I swung around and put all my weight on the forest side as the bear hit the tree again and it toppled through the lodgepole and aspen, the branches beating me half to death. It crashed into the forest floor and I hit hard. My right shoulder went numb and I knew it was dislocated.

No time. No time.

I jumped up and ran for the sharp berm that marked the dirt road winding the ridge. I scrambled up it, screaming at the pain in my shoulder but spurred by the sound of trees snapping and giant paws digging into the dirt behind. I reached the top and did not break stride but cut right and hurled down the road, back towards the trailhead and the Rangers, the only chance I had. Trees fell beside me as the bear kept pace below the berm, even gaining a lead, as I held my shoulder together with my left hand, crying, praying that a Ranger was tooling about making rounds. Please God ...

A glint in the distance. Sunlight off a windshield. Holy Jesus and all His Angels.

I ran, Jesse Owens ran, the hounds-of-hell-on-my-heels ran, and the crashing trees down the berm fell behind.

The Ranger must have seen me coming because he was standing at the front tire, arms akimbo, in complete astonishment. "What in Sam Hill happened to you?" he called.

I did look a mess: half naked, welts and blood crisscrossing my body, shoulder at an impossible angle. "Bear!" I screamed as I raced towards him.

I was close enough to see his puzzled look. "What bear?"

I stopped. I turned. The road behind me was empty. The berm beside me was still. I shook my head in amazement and headed towards the Ranger. "I'm telling you, there was a bear. Satan's bear."

"Now are you sure you just didn't fall off that?" the Ranger was amused, pointing up the other side of the road where the ridge continued its climb towards the Divide.

"No. Bear," I said, getting closer, gasping, thinking that I had made it. I was going to get out of this ...

The bear came flying off the upper ridge where the Ranger had just pointed and slammed into the side of the Jeep, rolling it over the Ranger, who barely had time to look at the commotion before the truck flattened him. The Jeep went over the berm, crashing into the trees down there, leaving the smooshed Ranger feebly trying to regain his feet. The bear swiped the Ranger's head clean off, shooting it past my ear like a cannon shot, the trailing line of blood slamming into my eyes and almost blinding me. The bear then stood full upright and dropped down, pulling the Ranger's chest apart with his claws, reaching in and yanking the Ranger's heart into the air. He caught it in his jaws on the fall and swallowed it in one gulp. Blood poured down the bear's face and all over his chest.

He stood back up, thrust his muzzle heavenward, opened his maw and roared triumph, lust, battle; a roar a million years old, heard a million times in places far more primitive, before the moon coalesced and new stars settled, before the two-legged smart animal figured out fire and how to sharpen a stick.

There were answering roars from the lower berm.

On the upper ridge was a trail starting at the road's shoulder, and if I remembered this right ... I bolted for it.

The bear dropped his head and watched me, unconcerned, the Ranger's blood already drying on his fur. He picked up the Ranger and hurled him off the side of the road to his waiting mates, went to all fours, and began a slow lope after me.

I stood, waiting. I wanted him after me. But he had to come much faster and madder, if this was going to work. "You fucking bastard!" I yelled from the slope of the trail, reached down with my good hand and heaved a good-sized rock at him, crying out from the pain. It cracked him in the nose, lucky shot, and the bear sat back, blinked, stood upright, bent himself double at the waist and gave me the most savage, hate filled roar it could muster.

Good.

I scrambled up the trail, watching as the bear took about four steps, dropped, roared its hate at me again, and then charged. I dug in, screaming at what this was doing to my shoulder and raced up the slope to where it peaked in the trees. There was a very sharp drop here, the Divide, and my momentum carried me into the scree that cascaded down the slope to a cliff overlooking a thirty-foot fall onto another ridge, first in a series all the way to the river below. I was upended by the loose soil and began a tumbling slide to the edge. I could not gain control and I desperately scrambled about seeking purchase, ripping my already ripped shoulder almost completely out, almost fainting from the pain.

The bear came over the ridge way too fast and immediately knew it, digging backwards and trying to set his paws but he had too much weight and too much momentum. He was a one-creature landslide, rocks and dirt riding with him and he almost fell backwards in a frantic effort to stop. All he did was gain speed. Gain on me. He was going to carry me with him if I didn't get out of the way.

At the edge of the cliff was a tangle of ivy and thorn and I turned in my slide and ran my destroyed arm underneath it as I cleared the edge and hurtled into space. I yanked at the tangle, pain be damned, and it jerked me to the side as the bear rushed over. Our eyes met as the tangle swung me away from him and he swiped a great paw that removed half my other shoulder as he fell past, teeth bared and frothing in rage and frustration.

I gasped from the blow, but it was so heavy and fast I

didn't really feel it. The tangle arced me hard into a rock outcropping and I felt my leg break below the knee. I was hurting too much for that to make much difference, though, as the tangle pendulumed back to its origin. My hand slipped and there was a shower of dirt and it felt like the tangle was going to come loose and drop me on the rocks and that would be all she wrote but, no, no, it held. I looked down.

The bear bounced hard, taking on angles he shouldn't have, and rolled, thrown from rock to rock, great gouts of blood exploding from his mouth, raging but helpless, and was carried to the next cliff and went over, lost to sight. But not sound. He roared. Defiance, heartbreak, defeat, a sound loud and echoing and tracing his fall to the other side of the country.

I was so numb that climbing was not a problem. I sat on the edge of the scree, exhausted, panting, stunned by the silence more than anything, then threw my head back and made my own roar. Triumph, lust, battle, a roar a million years old, heard a million times in places far more primitive.

That pretty much ended the numbness. In agony, I turned.

The other bears were arranged at the top of the scree in a semi-circle, sitting, quiet. Browns, blacks, Kodiak, maybe a polar, I couldn't be sure. I worked up to my good leg, watching them. There was nothing I could do. They'd be on me, no matter where I turned, and I was too torn up to run or fight. I braced. But they just sat. Eventually, one nudged a branch down the slope and, cautiously, fearfully, I grasped it as it slid past. The bears, one by one, stood, regarded me for a moment, then lumbered over the ridge.

I used the branch as a crutch and made my way back to camp and the ambulance is here now. They have shot me up with something, but I can still see clearly. Movement in the woods.

My court.

They will follow and, at night, they will stalk the circle of my home, a vague shadow in an alley, a blur in a distant parking lot, a homeless person here and there disappearing and an offering on my porch in the morning. A challenger will arise. We will meet on this ridge next year and we will battle.

I will remain king. Or I will not.

*Original version in Ezine *Bewildering Stories*. Issue 435

Angel Eyes

Right in my face, the vampire I've hunted the last twenty years. And me with no cross or garlic or holy water.

Great.

"Robert," Fang Boy hisses, licking a black tongue at me, the stench of rotted blood on his breath, "you're mine."

He's right, I am. "Must be a pretty good moment for you," I say.

He laughs, if you can call the wheezing snort typical of the species a laugh. If they had anything approaching a sense of humor, too. "Oh, Robert, it is, it is. Or, it's about to be." Another lick of the lips.

Great.

I look around. There are some high casement windows along the top walls of this warehouse, glowing red with the last moments of sunset. At least fifteen feet in the air, so no way. Besides, moron, it's sunset.

"Desperation, Robert?" Needletooth follows my gaze. "You wish to try for it?" he steps aside and flourishes his cape. "Please. Do so. I'll give you a head start. One, two ..." he goes to ten quite slowly, but I'm not stupid.

Usually.

"All this time, Robert. How could you be so stupid?"

I shrug, "Question I've asked myself."

"Weren't expecting me to be here?" He cocks a pencil thin eyebrow. "This was just reconnaissance?"

I say nothing. I'm not giving him the satisfaction.

"Ah," he nods, knowingly.

Bastard.

I'd been on the other side of town checking out a more likely warehouse and stopped by here spur of the moment. I'd figured out Fangface's modus about ten years ago; he liked abandoned storage units near a big river or bay. Odd for a vampire, as much as they hate running water, but good camouflage, in that respect. This particular warehouse didn't fit the profile — on a miasmic swamp with a chained entrance too close to main roads. And there was the dog. So I was looking at it for myself. Had no clue he was here.

Dammit.

"Tsk, tsk, Robert," Batboy shakes an admonishing finger, "you should know by now to expect anything."

"I'll take it under advisement. Where's Carson?" I look around, expecting the familiar to come out of the dark swinging an ax, and I don't mean a Stratocaster.

"Nearby," Toothsome grins.

Bull. This time o' day, Carson's out grabbing victims. Drac here didn't like taking risks, so he sent the hired help out to ambush nubiles and drag them back for his leisurely draining. More modus, always leading me to him.

"So you're here alone," I say more smugly than I feel, hoping I get a good reaction.

I do.

Vlad frowns, "I did not say that."

"Didn't have to," I retain the smugness, hoping it covers the bluff. Then I smile, hoping to enhance it.

Which it did. Alarmed, Nos wraps one hand around my throat and pins me to the wall then looks wildly about, searching for an attacker. His grip tightens and I gag for air as he brings his face inches away. "No one there, Robert. Did you actually think that would work?" Since I was pretty much throttled, I couldn't respond with trademark smart-alec patter along the lines of 'it being worth a shot.' He squeezes a little tighter and I figure this is it when he suddenly throws me to his feet.

"Not so easy, Robert," he says, "not for you." Again, I'd love to give a snarky response, maybe 'don't trouble yourself,' but breathing is my priority.

He steps back and taps a bony finger on his lantern jaw, "What should I do with you? Something to commemorate our years together." His eyes suddenly glow and he hauls me up by the throat, just as I am getting my breath back. "That's it!" he crows. "Your wife and daughter!"

Flashback. Three nights after burying Louise, dead suddenly of pernicious anemia ("We just don't understand it," the docs said), a noise from upstairs. There, my undead wife, hissing as she lapped the blood from our ten-year-old daughter's torn throat. "She's coming with me, Robert!" crash out the window, cradling Lisbeth.

"I'm thinking," Feratu says, "that we should first make you a woman," he grabs my manhood with his claws, which is definitely not conducive to catching your breath. "And then," as he hurls me, almost unconscious from both throat and scrotum grab, to my back, "tear off your legs." He kneels on my chest. "You know, height of a child?" He grins.

Great.

"Thought you'd be more interested in turning me." I'm not making conversation, just stalling. Fortunately, bloodsuckers are a talkative bunch.

"Who says I won't?" the grin gets wider. "It would be quite amusing to watch you pull along slavering after meat." That's what we are, meat. He drops his face an inch from mine. "And, Robert, you would."

Oh, here we go, the old 'woe is me I'm a vampire and I thirst' crap. I roll my eyes, "Please kill me before the violins start."

He sits back up, frowning. Like I said, no sense of humor. "Upon reflection, I think I shall, Robert. Keeping you with me, despite the entertainment, may not be wise. Your family has shown a disturbing lack of loyalty."

He is, of course, referring to Lisbeth. After dispatching her mother when they'd returned from an all-night feed, I sat down beside my weeping daughter as she clung to the now peaceful body of my wife. "Lisbeth," I whispered, "who did this to you?" She told me, and, as a gift, I let her glimpse the first rose of dawn. The worst death for a vampire is sunrise, and I wasn't going to let her suffer so, a second later, I drove a hawthorn stake through her heart and lopped off her head, then burned her and her mother to ash, soaked them in garlic and holy water, sealed the whole mess in her mother's coffin with wafer and re-interred them in Louise's grave.

Do less, they come back.

"Or," and he brightens, sort of a rare vampire look,

"I could just call the police." Not a joke, that, and it's my turn to frown. The cops had to blame somebody for the bloody mess in Lisbeth's room, even without a body. And since I'm now linked to scores of other bloody messes across the country in pursuit of Yorga here, they'd just throw away the key. Especially if I explain.

He actually thinks about it for a moment before shaking his head. "No, no, you're far too resourceful to leave alive."

"Well, thank you!"

He actually chuckles. "Robert, I must say, you have made the years interesting."

"Gonna miss me?"

His smile is cruel. "For about a minute."

"And yet you carry the reminders," I almost break into *The Boxer*, which would have prompted my instant death. I have a terrible singing voice.

His face goes mad as I look rather pointedly at his right side, where I'd managed to pin him to a wall with a Bowie knife in a St. Louis warehouse before Lemuel, Carson's predecessor, fought me off. I'd gutted Lemuel for that and left him, screaming, for the rats.

"You've come very close, Robert. You've been very lucky, but no more." His eyes redden, "And before you die, I will definitely see you as a woman and a child." He rears back, groping for my boys.

Which I am waiting for. While incredibly strong and incredibly fast, vamps are incredibly light. All that incorporeality and flying around, you see. About the only advantage humans have mano-a-mano is leverage, unless they get their hands on you then no amount of leverage will stop them from driving their talons straight through your body. Which is what he should have done instead of being all uber-vicious and petty and pontificating. Go for the kill. But Feratus just got to make a point.

So, I scissor, whipping my legs up and over just as he grabs the jewels. He flies across the room, giving only enough of a tug to make me yelp, but not incapacitate. I keep the scissor flowing up to my feet and off like a shot for the door. Working out pays off.

I'd learned, after a few tangles with Morbius and his buddies, that the biggest mistake is stopping to admire your handiwork. Vamps have extremely fast reactions and taking a second to, oh say, exult after throwing one down an elevator shaft is a sure-fire way to have it right back at you, fastened to your throat before you've stopped smiling. So, ordinarily, I don't look back, but this time, I couldn't help it.

He is right on me, silent, which is scarier than his screaming. Eyes scarlet, canines and front fangs extended, arms out and his cloak flapping in the breeze (yeah, affectation, but half of vamping is image). He is flying about three feet off the floor, and my sudden burst of terror spurs me to Jamaican track team speeds.

But, there is just no way I'm going to make it, not without unexpected help.

Which I get.

I am already in Barnabas' grasp, steps away from the door, when it flies open. "Hey, boss!" Carson, framed there, calls out, a pair of nubiles slung over his shoulders, "look what I brung ..."

He never gets to finish because I lower my head and barrel straight into him, Lestat hanging on my back. Familiars are not immortal, just sustained, the need to slosh about in daylight ensuring they retain that status until the master tires of them (likely), rewards them with turning (unlikely), or they get killed (most likely). So, my open field tackle has the desired effect.

"Oof!" he whooshes as I fold him like a jacknife right out the door, forcing Undead Fred off me as Carson drops the girls like two sacks of potatoes. They're in coma, so that didn't hurt 'em (much) and has the immediate benefit of severely distracting Stake Bait, who stands above the girls, wavering. Vamps just can't help themselves. Carson also has the good sense to crack his skull wide open as he falls, geysering blood. Another big distraction — so many menu choices.

Which means I have gained a couple of minutes. Two options: go for my car, with its trunk load of stakes, garlic spray, holy water vials, machete, wafer, crosses, what have you, or go for the dog.

No contest.

I spin away from the parking lot and beeline for the corner, taking it on one leg. I look back to see He Who Avoids Sunlight rising from Carson's body, trailing blood down his face. Good strategy. He needs an energy burst to finish me off and Carson is lying there, a convenient Snickers bar. The girls can wait until he's done turning me inside out.

Which, incidentally, he's really in the mood to do.

"ROOOOBEEERT!" he screams and flies straight up, out of my sight. Uh oh, trying to cut me off through the air.

I hit overdrive down the lane, watching him gain over the warehouse roof. Two more buildings to go, just two, and if I can just...

Wham! His feet plow into my back, driving me into a head-first power slide. I pile into the wall, my feet going over top and forcing me into a somersault. Head spinning, I sit up, back against the wall.

It is full on dark now, but there's pretty good lighting back here. Mr. Moon-tan is in the middle of the lane gazing down at me, Carson dripping from his lips. "Robert," he says, "running away? How futile."

"Can't blame a guy for trying."

"Oh yes, yes I can, Robert," he snarls, "especially when you kill my servant!"

"Actually, you did that."

"But you caused it," more snarling and I toy with the idea of getting into this whole cause-and-effect argument; you know, I wouldn't have been here to kill Carson if you hadn't taken my family, etc., etc. But then he'd go into all this nature-of-the-business crap and I shoulda just mourned and moved on instead of seeking revenge, yadda yadda. So, no, think I'll just get to the main point. "You know, Tomb Fool, I just did you a huge favor."

"Insults," he shakes his head, "classy, Robert. And you've done me no favors."

"Yeah, I have. See," and I shift my feet to get a little more comfortable, "I rid you of a bad valet."

He stares at me. "Carson was a trial," he agreed, "but they all are. It's very inconvenient to replace them. Because of that, I'm going to tear off your arms and legs and let you bleed to death."

"Not my gonads?"

He grins, "Them, too."

"Darn it," I say, snapping a regretful finger, "and I had a date later."

"Funny," but he's not smiling. His talons elongate, as does his fangs, his eyes glow with hellfire and he starts the mad vampire rush – in four steps he'll be on me.

In two steps, though, he hesitates, sensing something wrong, because I'm just sitting there calmly, not reacting at all. In three, he tries to pull up, knowing something is definitely wrong. Could be the sound of rapidly approaching paws and the jangling of collar tags.

The dog barrels around the corner, coming to a screeching halt dead between Leech Teeth's outstretched hands and me. It sits right there, staring up at him. Ordinarily, not a problem – Blood Breath whacks it out of the way then whacks me; after all, it's just your standard junkyard, underfed, mongrelized Labrador ...

Except for the two white eyebrows, what we in the trade call angel eyes.

Casually, I get to my feet, stopping to pat the dog's head. It doesn't move, fixated on Corpse Puppet like a Shriner on a pole dancer. "Wassamadder?" I look at Polidori. "Dog got your tongue?"

You can see the struggle, Fanger's worm-tube excuse for veins pulsing and writhing as he strains mightily to move something, a toe, a thumb, anything to break the spell. Fat chance. The only way to do it is move the dog, and since I wasn't going to, someone else has to, you know, like Carson?

"Bet you regret that snack about now," I can't help rub it in. "But, maybe not. I mean, what kind of idiot slave picks a sanctuary with this," I pat the dog again, "running around?"

"Dis. Trac. Tion," he wheezes through clenched teeth, er, fangs, the worm-tubes working frantically.

I stare at him, which elicits a mesmer attempt that I easily brush off, "You mean, you knew about it?"

He nods imperceptively, which must have taken extraordinary effort. Gotta admit, tough guy. "But, the dog's why I wanted this place ..." and it all comes clear. I start laughing. "Oh man, too much. Just like you always pick running water, you thought I'd look for you elsewhere. No way a crafty vamp like you would hole near an angel-eyed dog. Right?"

The rage floods his face and, for a half second, I think he'll generate enough to break free, but the dog is strong. "I get it. I really do. Don't kill the dog; that'd alert me. Have Carson pen it up while you're feeding. You're not bothered, I search elsewhere, you drain the city. Quite clever." I began the slow Handclap of Irony, which pushes even more rage but, strong dog. "Hoisted, as we say, on one's own petard."

Man, he is really fighting. The life urge of a vamp is downright psychotic, which, in my rather informed opinion, has much to do with their post-death activities. No easy acceptance of the Veil among these Undead prospects, no sir, not even that grudging sense of the inevitable, which is how the rest of us view our ultimate demise. That's why they come back, corrupt and stinking and screaming for blood. That's why you have to take measures, so they don't steal loved ones and you end up spending the rest of a craven life following their stench, slaughtering their brood, seeking respite.

Measures.

I walk around the dog so I don't bump it and search the front of the building. Lots of scrap wood around but most not suitable so it takes me a bit to find a good candidate. All the time, Gary Oldman is groaning and whining as he struggles against the dog, which is more than holding its own, and I suppose I could just leave them both for sunrise. My luck, though, a stray cat'll stroll by.

No. This time, no slip-ups, no last-second escapes. No more decades spent hunting and huddled and broke and alone.

This. Ends. Now.

I position myself behind nightstalker and measure the distance. "You don't mind," I speak softly to Drakul's back, "if I savor the moment?" Judging by his whimpers, he does mind, and his moaning and shaking quadruples. I glance worriedly at the dog, but what a trouper. It just lowers its head and stares more intently, if that's possible. I heft the board scrap, pointy end at my target.

Measure twice, cut once.

I drive the end of the board with all my considerable strength right through and out his chest. That breaks the spell, of course, and he whirls around the board, snarling, while the dog runs off yelping. Like I said, tough guy, and he nicks my shoulder with a talon as I duck. Doesn't matter. The quivering end of the board is black with his rotted blood, sure sign I'd struck home. No arterial spray with these things; they just ooze, and if you hit anywhere but the heart, you don't even get that. So, I'm exulting a bit, even more when he sinks to his knees, the fight gone out of him. My God, Who abandoned me those twenty years ago, is it finally, now, here, over?

Well, not quite.

He's not dead, er, un-Undead, I mean, dispatched to the lower circles of hell where he belongs, yet. That'll take a little more doing and he remains dangerous so I remain out of reach. But I am here, and this has happened, and off in the distance I hear Lisbeth weeping.

"Robert," he gasps, a feeble hand pulling at the wood and I worry he'll dislodge it, but no, it's in there pretty good. Nice work, I mentally backslap myself. "Robert, please."

"Be right back," I say and turn on my heel, ignoring his cries for mercy. "Don't go anywhere," sung over my shoulder. Yeah, a bit nasty, but this is the end of an era. I'm almost whistling when I get to the car, feeling light, almost incorporeal, yuk yuk. I grab what I need, including a set of noise-canceling headphones because plasma pooches can mesmerize with their voices, too.

Since we still have some time together, I'm not taking any chances.

'Course he's not there when I get back, which I expected. I'd be sorely disappointed if he didn't at least make the effort. Blood trail is easy to follow and the only surprise is how far under the building he's managed to crawl. The force is strong with this one, Obi Wan. No way I'm going in after so I shine the light on his cue ball, gnashing-teeth, pumpkin-of-a-head, fire the grapple, and drag him out by his legs, Count Chocula screaming the whole time. Oops, sorry, wadja say? Can't hear a thing with these headphones.

I pull him into the middle of the lane, staying out of reach. He writhes and claws at me, still trying to get that board out, but unsuccessful. I shove a cross in the dirt at the compass points around him, each one causing a blood curdling howl, or, I'm assuming they do, by his twisted neck, agonized face, and wide-open mouth. Can't hear. Headphones.

I stand back, brush my hands to get the dirt off, and survey my handiwork. He's in a fetal position, crying, those crosses hammering him into submission, the board robbing him of his strength and speed. I tap my chin with my finger, "What should I do with you? It should be something to commemorate our years together, yes?" Tap, tap, tap, then a raised, dramatic finger, "Let's do something you haven't done in, what, a couple of centuries?" I grab my pack, unfold the camp chair, turn on the PSP (*The Last Vampire*, natch), and drop some crystal.

That'll keep me up and alert, although I tend to get a little crazy with it. I lean forward, "Let's watch the sunrise together, shall we?" and settle back in my chair.

It looks like he screams, "Noooo!"

Can't tell, headphones.

*Original version in *Dark Gothic Magazine*

The Absence of Land

Eddie wasn't surprised when Dad walked out of the woods (or, where the woods used to be), stepped up next to him, and leaned on the fence. Startled, maybe, but not surprised. Dad's spirit was tied to the land. Why should it leave?

"Hello, son," Dad said.

Eddie nodded, wary. "Hi Dad. You look good."

"Thanks." Dad eyed him critically. "You've put on weight."

Eddie patted his stomach and grinned, "I eat good."

"And get no exercise."

"Yes I do. I go to the gym. I run."

"That ain't the same thing, son." Dad turned away

and stared over the field; he was hawk-eyed and weathered by decades of Iowa. "Sorghum."

"Yes." Eddie reached through the metal rails and gently stroked a blade of it, green, rich, vital.

"Followed by wheat." Dad's tone was contemptuous. "Modern farming."

"They've got new techniques, Dad. No allelopathy."

"Do you notice, son, that you say 'they'?"

"Dad ..."

Dad faced Eddie. His eyes were different. Dad always had vision; he could sweep the farm and take in the corn's slightest color change, a centimeter's growth on the beans, which way the cows were facing, and immediately know everything's status. Now he saw other things.

"Why, Edward?" Dad asked it softly.

Eddie never had to answer that question from Dad. Mom and the uncles, of course, but that wasn't the same thing. He did go to the cemetery and stand over Dad and explain, albeit in his own terms, and not in a way Dad would accept. Eddie's words always failed. But he had no others. "It's all changed, Dad."

He cocked his head. "Tell me how it's all changed, son."

"You can't make a living that way anymore."

"What do you mean by 'living'?"

"Dad ..." Eddie shook his head, exasperated. He'd

had this argument with Mom and the uncles already. "It's different. Kids need things. My kids needed things."

"All kids need are the same things this needs." Dad gestured at the field, "Sun, water, space, and nutrition. What they *want*, is a different matter."

"Not anymore, Dad. Wants in your time are needs today. Life is more ..." he searched for the best word, "... complicated."

"Only because you say it is. Doesn't mean it really is." Dad turned back to the field, gesture of finality.

"Dad, no one can make a living farming anymore."

"No one?" Dad glanced mildly at him.

"Well, alright." Eddie waved an impatient hand. "Some do. The co-ops, I know, everyone told me that. But eking it out year to year, terrified of the weather, always one season behind on the loan ..." He shook his head. "That's no kind of life."

"The house had no mortgage, son." Gentle tone. "That is, until you put one on it."

"We needed new equipment, Dad."

"And new clothes. And Playstations. And private schools. And tutors, too, I reckon."

Eddie's breath came out slow. There it was, Dad's favorite technique, the Ironic List, dispassionate, non-accusatory, yet as devastating as a pointed finger.

"Yes." Eddie was mad now. "Those things. And others. Like college. Like weddings. Like grandchildren." Two could do this.

Dad nodded, "Those things, too. Which we had."

It was like a punch in the stomach. Eddie slumped against the metal fence — not the white picket one he had to paint every year — to get his air back. "I'm not you," he finally said.

"I know." Dad's voice dropped even more, if that was possible. "I don't mean to imply you should be. But," his blue-now-forever eyes blazed suddenly, locked on Eddie, "you stood right here, right next to me, and you said you'd live here forever."

"I was fourteen."

"Don't have to be much older to know what's true."

Eddie shut his eyes, held them, let the sorrow flow. "All right."

Dad was still there when he opened them. "Tell me, Eddie, why do you keep coming back?"

"It was home, Dad."

Dad looked behind them at the field of soy. "Was, Eddie. All plowed under. So, why? They could arrest you for trespassing."

"They won't."

"Your suit, your Cadillac, will stop them?" Dad smiled. "They can do what they want. They don't, though, because it would be pathetic."

"That's not fair."

"Then, tell me, son," those eyes again, "why do you

keep coming back?"

"Why do you?"

Dad laughed, his real laugh, rich and full and alive, alive, alive. God's Own Chuckle, Mom used to call it. "Oh, Edward, I am this place. Always will be. Besides," he winked, "am I really here?"

"You look real enough."

"I look like what you want. I sound like what you want. I'm even using your words and what you remember of mine. Is it real?"

Slowly, Eddie pushed a finger at Dad's arm, felt the slight resistance, incorporeal. He took a step back, frowning. "Don't think it matters."

Dad just smiled. "Question still stands, son."

Eddie lowered himself and took a handful of the soil. It was black as ever, probably more so now, thanks to Monsanto. "I think I screwed up."

"It calls to you, doesn't it?"

Eddie clutched the soil into a moist clump. Nights, Betty unconscious while he prowled the house, stepping onto the veranda, cool granite tiles under his feet making them itch because it wasn't grass and dirt and direct contact with the earth. Had to walk out through the patio and past the pool and barbecue pit across the flagstone just to dig a toe down.

"It calls to everyone. It still calls to me, son."

A sob escaped Eddie, surprising him. He stood, the

dirt turning to rock in his hand. "Dad."

"It's all right, son. It ain't you. The spirit has changed. The men of commodity, they changed it all."

"But Dad, I just feel so ..." He couldn't find the word.

"Disconnected." Dad took in a breath. "I know. Everyone does now. They don't know why. They think they need a raise or a title or headlines but what they need," and Dad's hand shot out, corporeal now, fiercely seizing Eddie's hand and crushing his fingers, binding them into the clump, the earth seeping into his blood, his heart, "is this."

Eddie gasped, squeezing his eyes shut. The pain. "Dad, you're hurting me!"

"No," Dad's voice was far away and Eddie opened his eyes and Dad *was* far away, standing where the woods used to be, the squirrel woods where they all, Dad and he and Sloan and Frankie and Carol and, yes, Betty, took their silly BB guns and missed more tree rats than they annoyed, and the day the buck walked out, majestic and crowned, and looked at him, so astonishing he could not bring the rifle up. And Dad had whispered, "Let him go, son."

And where the chestnuts fell and were gathered for midnight roasting, and you walked through to the north field because there, right there, you could see the ecliptic and measure the seasons, and the wind caressed you and the growth, the pure life, bowed to you and bid welcome.

"You hurt yourself," carried on the wind that mentioned summer and, for a moment, Dad stood against the ghost woods, the ghost house, ghost fence.

And was gone.

Eddie leaned against the industrial slats and measured the sorghum with his eye and snorted a contempt for laboratory farmers who forced a chemical compatibility. Don't you know you put a food crop — corn is best — between the breads? He leaned his head back, eyes zenith, and measured the angle and the time until equinox and thought of harvest moons.

Then he walked back to his car and drove two hours home.

*Original version in EZine *Bewildering Stories*, 320

Face to Face

"I'm sorry," the tweedy woman said, "We can't release those records."

Show time.

"Well, actually, you can," Lane kept his voice smooth, lawyer smooth. "Release of local adoption records is at the holder's discretion. You have only to satisfy the state requirements, and I believe this document," – Lane handed the forgery to her – "suffices."

The tweedy woman, Mrs. Conover, black, fiftyish, officious, the air of Protecting Our Children about her, took it with an air of ready rejection. Lane inwardly sneered. Was it civic duty? Or just the power?

Mrs. Conover finished reading, "I understand the adoptee is deceased ..." Her practiced Voice of Regret kicked in.

No, he isn't, Lane flashed a thought at her, *he's sitting right in front of you.* She didn't catch it, of course; lesser beings didn't have his gifts, like the reading of expressions. Hers was saying she bowed to the gods of statute, and statute said no release under any circumstances.

Time to introduce a more powerful god.

"Perhaps this will ease any concerns?" Lane handed her the second forgery and watched as she read, her eyes widening.

Texture, Calvin had said, *that's why fakes get spotted. Not enough texture. People think they can knock something together on PhotoShop and fool somebody. Amateurs.*

Lane had used the stylus, adding weight to the signature and watermark until both were perfect. Judging by Mrs. Conover's expression, it was passing muster. He breathed deep, pressing a sharp thumbnail into his leg to keep it from bouncing. *Stay calm. Only one shot at this.*

"Well ..." Mrs. Conover hesitated, "I suppose if the Senator assures us anonymity ..."

Oh my God, it was working! "He does." Lane remained lawyer smooth, proud of his self-control. "Your agency will never be cited."

She still looked doubtful. Lane produced the Senator's business card, another forgery, but a lot easier to do. "If you want, you can verify all of this." And he gave her the card with an expectant smile and an encouraging nod at the phone. *Don't call, don't call, don't call*, he chanted under his breath.

She considered, looking at the card and the phone. Lane braced for sudden flight. She compared the card against the two letters and the two letters against each other

Calvin: *Three pieces. Two makes them suspicious. Three don't.*

She looked up. "It's just for genealogical research?"

Lane sang. She'd bought it. They were now in what Calvin called 'validation.'

"That's all," Lane smiled and cocked his head and put out expansive, innocent hands. *Nothing to worry about, Ma'am. You're validated.*

She stood. "I'll be a few moments."

"Take your time," Lane said casually while inside he screamed *Hurry up!*

She was back in twenty agonizing, world-ending, someone called the cops and they're outside right now, minutes. No cops. Just her. And a manila folder. She kept it out of view, just a last few moments of torture. "You understand you can't have this," she warned.

He nodded vigorously, "Yes, Ma'am. I only need to take a couple of notes."

"So who is the Senator's friend?" she asked, still holding it back which made Lane too anxious and, for a moment, he looked at her blankly. *What the hell are you talking about? Oh. Right.*

"Now, Mrs. Conover," he said it conspiratorially, "this is a discreet matter. If I told you, I'd be violating a trust." Left unsaid was her own reluctance to violate trusts, a meeting of common interests. So let's be sports about this, hey? *Give me the goddamn file, you stupid bitch!*

"The Senator had only to call us."

She wasn't suddenly suspicious, she was curious. What high and mighty person had a quiet need to check ancestors? *Make them think they're part of it,* Calvin had said. Lane leaned forward and dropped his voice to a whisper, "Let's just say, presidential aspirations are involved?" He raised his eyebrows and glanced off to the side.

She handed him the file and sat back, watching. He held it for a moment, which is about the only time of reverence the play allowed. Across the top, his name, his real name.

He opened it, deliberately keeping his eyes steady. But he lost a bit of control and shakily leafed through documents until ...

There.

He had never seen his birth certificate, only a Report of Birth in Lieu of Certificate. Sure, he had all the ones he and Calvin made, but this was the real deal. This was him. Father: Unknown. Mother ...

The name of God on children's lips. He held his breath as he read:

Mary Lloyd Vincent. A birth date 20 years and some months before his own. A birthplace, Pembrook, New Jersey. An address in California, current as of the certificate.

Hello, Mom.

～ ～

It started when he was about eleven. Before then, he played with his three sisters, their pale blonde hair flying, their blue eyes sparkling as he, their only brother, chased and tagged and swam and biked and screamed the high hilarity of summers and afternoons and Christmases and weekends. It was perfect and golden and innocent. Until Henry.

"So how come you look so different?" Henry the Bully, bent down and scrutinizing him, "how come you all dark? You Rican?"

"Nooo," Lane had used the kid tone of ridicule, "I ain't. I'm the boy, stupid. I got the dark hair and eyes."

"From who?" Henry snorted. "You parents as lily-ass white as you sisters. You must be Rican or something. You're weird lookin'."

They fought, Lane getting the worst of it. "Mom," he wailed as she bandaged him, "Henry said I'm weird lookin' because I'm dark and the girls are all blonde." And he saw it, the quick look away, the hesitation. "What?" he'd asked.

"Nothing," she said, "it's because you're the boy, that's all." But her hug was tentative.

"You're just the boy," Dad had said but he looked

away, too, and Lane was suspicious. He searched filing cabinets until he found the documents. His sisters had genuine certificates that listed Mom and Dad. All he had was a Report in Lieu.

"What's this?" he'd asked. "How come it's different than Beth's and Jo's and Meg's?"

"You're adopted," his parents said.

Speechless, he listened to a tale of sisters who did not carry the family name and the need for a son to do so and the going to a lawyer who found the agency who arranged his placement and they just loved him so and he was like their real son ...

He raised a hand and stopped them. "So who's my mother?"

"We don't know," they said and they both looked sincere and giving and open and Lane wanted to smash their faces.

"I'm adopted," he told Henry.

"So you are Rican. And your mother was a whore," Henry crowed. Lane blinked, picked up a brick, and opened Henry's head. Sixty-seven stitches and six months of rehab. Lane got six weeks in Juvy.

When he got out, he went to his, er, parents. "I want to know who my mother is."

"We can't tell you that."

"Why?"

"Well, first, we don't know, and second, *we're* your parents." Dad. All business.

Lane burnt the house down, hoping to take them all but he only managed to get Jo. At least one of them was now dark, if only on one side of her face.

They put him in hospitals at first. He resisted, which got him medications and restraints and solitary. He finally realized resistance was stupid. All they wanted was a sense that all their hand-wringing concern for his well-being was leading somewhere. So he developed a practical ability to con and used it to get out of the hospitals and into halfway houses, and from there into lots of foster homes. He got quite a schooling in the various adult personalities, from the overly compassionate, to the indifferent, to the cruel. He tested and lost and tested and won and learned.

A lot.

And he spent far too much time studying himself. One of the overly compassionate sprung for counseling and that's where Lane first heard of the Oedipus complex. "You have an unhealthy fixation on your mother," the bearded, glasses-wearing geek said. Well, duh. Fathers could be anyone, but you had only one mother.

Identity, the Holy Grail of Adoption. Lane knew that if he saw her, scrutinized her, compared himself to her, then everything would fall into place. Beard geek didn't think so, but that didn't matter because he was only a factor for about three sessions, when the money ran out.

He'd met Calvin while doing two years for fraud. It was the best two years of his life. Calvin was doing forty-five and figured his counterfeiting days were done and he needed an apprentice. Lane had some forgery skills. They fell in.

Their lovemaking was the usual prison type, tension release only, but Calvin truly liked him. "You've got real talent, kid," he'd say, pinching a bit of Lane's face, an act that would get anyone else shanked. He taught Lane everything. Lane told him everything.

"Say hi to your Mom for me," Calvin shook his hand the day Lane was paroled. Lane hugged him.

Father.

⁃ ⁃

It was a little town, this Ajo, California. Lane got off the bus, ticket courtesy of the old couple in Des Moines who had missed his deft movements and probably wouldn't miss their cards for at least another week.

Lane kept an inner smile as he used their American Express to buy a cheap suit, more hair lightener, and a gross pair of black horn-rimmed glasses. [Calvin: *Wear something stupid. That's all they'll remember.*] He traded the other cards for a badge blank and made a new set of credentials at Kinko's.

"Good morning, Ma'am," he said as he held the badge and credentials up to his face, typical goofball detective. "I'm looking for Mary Vincent." Outwardly, he oozed business.

Inwardly, he was an earthquake, staring hard at the older woman staring at him suspiciously from the cracked door. *Is that you, Mom?*

"*Quién? Qué quieres? No la conozca!*" and she made to slam the door but Lane already had his shoe in it. So, not her. Lane lapsed into playground Spanglish and the woman's suspicion relented enough that she, at least, didn't try to crush his toes. "*Alejandro!*" she called, "*véngate!*"

"What?" A petulant voice matched the petulant, torn-T-shirted teen who frowned at Lane through the door. "What you want, man?" He pronounced it 'mien.'

"I'm looking for Mary Vincent, Mary Lloyd Vincent?" Lane waved the badge in the punk's face. Distraction, intimidation.

He wasn't intimidated. "Do we look like our names are 'Vincent', man?" and he moved to slam the door.

"She used to live here," Lane just barely kept the desperation out of his voice.

"Not anymore," another move to slam.

"It would have been twenty years ago."

The teen eyed him balefully. "Go next door. That old guy's been here forever." And this time he did slam.

The old guy, fat, bewhiskered, rolls of him falling out of what Lane swore was the same T-shirt as the teen, *had* been there forever. "*Sí, la conocí.* She got busted. Prostitution. Went to jail. Don't know where she went after that. Why you ask?" and the old man scrutinized him and maybe there was a glimmer of recognition. Lane didn't stay long enough for it to spark.

So, Henry had been right.

⌣ ⌣

There were six Vincents listed in the Pembrook, New Jersey area. "Who?" they all responded to his query. "Not one of us." He went to the local high school and looked through yearbooks, but she wasn't there.

He sat in his car — reminder: steal another one tomorrow — in the parking lot of the White Dotte, some kind of luncheonette at the intersection of some kind of state routes, drumming his fingers on the steering wheel and idly sorting through the papers in the glove box for anything he could use.

So, what now? He shook his head. He could look up dear old Mom and Dad and pull out their fingernails until they gave the name of the adoption lawyer and then repeat the procedure until he got a more accurate fix on his mother. Messy. Time-consuming. And dangerous. He was about six steps ahead of the cops right now but, the longer this took, the more chance they'd get lucky, like run his plate while he was sitting here acting suspicious. Nervously, he glanced around and his eyes fell on a road sign.

Vincentown. 5 miles.

Vincent. Town.

No way.

He pulled out of the parking lot, breaking traction in

his sudden haste but no sirens so, okay. He followed the arrows and pulled up to the town hall.

"Mary Vincent's a pretty common name around here," the boozy redhead with the smoke-curdled skin snorted as she popped a Hershey's kiss from a bowl set on the counter (hand-printed sign: "Take One!) into her mouth.

"I figured," Lane looked properly abashed, "but she would have been born ..." and he gave the date and place.

"In Pembrook?" Boozy's eyes narrowed, "not Hollyhill? That's where the hospital is."

"No, Pembrook. And her full name was Mary Lloyd Vincent."

"Hmm, you know, that rings a bell."

Bingo. Mary Lloyd Vincent was born in the basement of her Uncle John Lloyd's house, located in the middle of Pembrook, when her mother went into sudden labor. Mary was home-schooled on the family farm about three miles out of Vincentown. "I remember her some," Boozy said, "She was real wild when she got about fifteen. Ran away a lot."

"Is she still here?" he tried to keep his voice casual.

"Could be," Boozy shrugged. "I haven't seen her in about twenty years, though. Farm's still in the family. Say, are you a relative? 'Cause, ya know," and Boozy squinted at him, "you sure got the look."

"No," he said hastily, "just doing research. Paper for college."

"Little old for college, ain'cha?"

Lane could have smacked himself. "Graduate studies," he said through a false smile. "Can I get directions?"

He was completely out of breath when he turned down the cedar-lined dirt driveway. A house, peeling white paint with gutters hanging haphazardly, brooded at the end, fallen-down garage next to it. Dizzy, Lane almost fell when he reached the porch. *Oh, God, oh God, after all these years, after all this searching, the Grail.* He knocked.

An old woman, one eye milky white to match her hair, dressed in a shiftless sack of a dress and smoking a giant cigar, yanked it open. "Wachawant?"

"Mary Vincent?" he steadied a hand on a porch column.

She puffed balefully at him. "No. I ain't your mother."

Lane's jaw dropped.

"Why so shocked?" Another puff. "You look just like her."

Something tight and painful suddenly loosed in Lane. "Where is she?" his voice was weak.

"Dead." The tight and painful thing screwed itself right back into place and he staggered. The old lady flourished the cigar. "The AIDS got her."

"Are you her ..." Lane took a stab, "mother?" Which

made her grandmother. A real grandmother.

"Ha!" The cigar punctuated her amusement. "Naw, I ain't your Maw-maw. I ain't a Vincent. They ain't no more Vincents. They all gone."

"But, they said the farm was still in their name."

"It is."

"So, then," Lane's confusion was evident.

Her eyes narrowed, "You ask a lot a questions."

Ah. Place to crash, off the books, no one really checking. Good con.

"So you gonna claim the place now?" she waved the cigar over the swamp-puddled and weed-grown yard, the rot taking the foundation even as Lane watched.

"Probably not," he said.

"Hmph," she grunted her satisfaction. "Good. Lots of back taxes on this place. You don't look like you could cover them."

Lane nodded. *Don't worry, Endora, your little hideaway is safe. For now.* "Tell me about her."

She shrugged. "Smarter than most. Your grands was these religious cultists. Real nuts, and she didn't like it much. Paid 'em back. Ran the GI's at Fort Dix. Had you." She one-eyed him.

"How do you know all that?"

She shrugged, "We were business partners." And she gave him a sly look. Her one eye was pretty expressive.

"So why'd she give me up?" Lane couldn't help sounding peevish.

She picked up on it. "Listen," her face darkened, "you be grateful for that. Saved your life. How you think you'd be if you grew up here?" She pointed at the malarial yard.

Grateful? He blinked. Be grateful? The painful thing twisted and hardened. *You just don't throw your children away, milk eye. You just don't.* His heart started to pound. She must have seen it because she grew alarmed.

"What did she look like?" His teeth were clenched.

"Get a mirror. That's her." She edged back a bit. "I ain't got any more for ya." And faster than her age would telegraph, she slammed and bolted the door.

Dammit! The rage roared through his head and arms and made them terrible. He slammed the door with both fists and felt it shake. "Goddamn bitch!" he bellowed, "Give me my mother!"

"You go away!" she shrieked. Lane measured the door. Couple of good kicks and it would come off the hinges and he'd have her pustule-laden liver-spotted neck in his hands. But she probably had a shotgun or, worse, some meth-head cooker hiding back there.

He whirled and stared at the car. Come flying at the house with it, take out the front, take her out at the same time. Then he'd have the whole place to search. Rage gripped his spine and head, blasting his senses, making him see the world red. Images flowed by: blonde sisters not his sisters, loving parents not his parents, his own darkness a beacon, marker, calling out his separation. He grabbed the sides of his head to squeeze it out, squeeze it all out, this shape under his skin, unknown, foreign, a cipher.

"Look in the mirror?" he turned and screamed at the house. "Look at what?" Someone lost, abandoned. No identity.

The blood-pounding lessened. He gasped, seeking air. The world resumed its colors and he felt the rage go back to its banks, settle around his heart. He breathed. All right, all right, forget the car. But, dammit all to hell! So close, so goddamn close!

"Do you have a picture, at least?" he asked the door.

"No," the tremulous voice betrayed her terror. He could use that. "You know," he called to Broomhilda, "I'll bet this place would burn real good." And he grinned.

"I know where she's buried!" a hasty response from the other side.

Lane cocked his head. "Go on."

"She was afraid of cremation. Got that from her parents. So she had a plot and some money set aside to make sure she got a real burial."

Lane pulled the Bic out of his pocket and snapped it near the door so she could hear. "Near you!" Her voice went up a notch. "Where you was placed with the agency!"

Lane took a step back. "What?"

"She wanted to be buried near you."

Lane stopped breathing.

"She felt real bad she had to give you up."

Mom. Mom, Mom ... It was mantra and something broke in Lane's stomach. "Tell me where," he whispered.

She did. My God, it was just one town over from home. "If you're lying," he said as he left, "it'll take you three days to die."

It took him three days to find her. The witch hadn't been real specific, but persistence, frenzied, insane persistence, paid off.

Midnight, a leprous, cloud-shrouded moon peeking at him, shocked. Lane flipped it off and sank the shovel into the mossy earth.

Time to get acquainted, Mom.

*Original version in EZine *Bewildering Stories*

About the Author

D. Krauss was born in Germany, adopted by a military family, and so became a US citizen in a roundabout way. He lived in Oklahoma and Alabama, somehow ending up in New Jersey where he lived every single Bruce Springsteen song. He joined the USAF, staying twenty years longer than intended. He has been a cotton picker, sod buster, painter of roads, surgical orderly, weatherman, librarian, special agent, analyst, and a bus driver. D's been married over 40 years (yep, same woman) and has a wildman bass guitarist for a son. You can reach him at http://www.dustyskull.com.

OTHER BOOKS BY D. KRAUSS

The Frank Vaughn Trilogy:

The Partholon Trilogy:

The Ship Trilogy

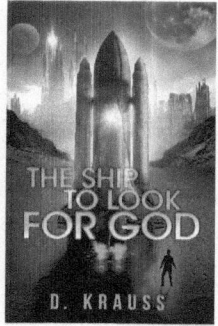  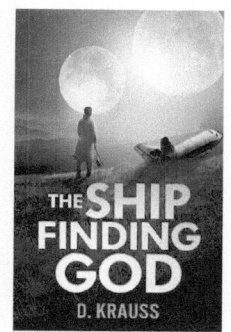

Story Collections

Young Adult

www.indiesunited.net/d-krauss

Cassandra Harris is a Seattle-born illustrator who graduated from North Seattle College with an Associate of Fine Arts (AFA) in arts. She's now based in Houston, where she's thriving her career as an illustrator. She's constantly stumbling into the next interesting book, so you can contact her at mae40221@gmail.com.

www.ingramcontent.com/pod-product-compliance
Lightning Source LLC
Chambersburg PA
CBHW020645180626
46816CB00003B/1134